LORD OF GOBLINS

MICHIEL WERBROUCK & HADI Y. BENDAKJI

TABLE OF CONTENTS

PROLOGUE

A shot was fired. The bullet flew towards its target, perfectly aimed. A smoking, empty shell ejected, its owner unblinking at the scene unfolding before him. What should have been a day of joy, a day of triumph against corruption, became a day of sorrow.

TARGET ELIMINATED: Leonard Erand Vandersteen (35), United Technocracy of Eurasia, Full Citizenship, Member of the United Council.

Leonard Erand Vandersteen would never get to finish his victory speech. A paragon of justice in the political world who just a few days prior had celebrated his thirty-fifth year of living on this earth, was now struggling against the icy grip of death.

Heh. You think it'll end with me, huh? thought Lev as his life began slipping away. *I can't blame you. As always, you're a bunch of shortsighted fools.*

Lev had prepared a contingency plan for this very situation. Upon his death, all national media outlets would be hijacked to broadcast all his rivals' dirty secrets—not the usual dirty secrets that politicians would hire foreign parties to spread, drawing eyes away from their recent activities, but all their secret prostitution rings, all their unknown crime syndicates, all their hidden deals with foreign parties, all their secret wars, and the worst, all their "fun" activities involving children who had gone missing in recent years.

He had wanted to reveal the truth sooner, but he needed the people's trust, as few would believe an unknown upstart over leaders they had been taught to believe and rely on. Over time, he had collected more and more evidence against them, and would have released everything once he had the power to repel their efforts to undermine him and cover the evidence back up. Not that he had been silent all this time—he had spread rumors via third parties across his own network to prevent them from discovering his efforts.

Lev could not help but grin. What should have been an act to cement their control over the government would ultimately lead to its collapse, and a new state would arise like a phoenix from its ashes.

A frantic man shoved his way forward. "Out of the way!" he shouted. "Lev!"

Though Lev's already blurry vision was darkening, he could never mistake this voice, whose owner had followed him through thick and thin all his life from the tender years of their childhood in the orphanage to the callous present. *Brutus,* he thought.

"It's not your time, man!" Brutus yelled. He turned to a woman just behind him. "Maria, call an ambulance!" He applied pressure to Lev's wound, but it was too late. Death demanded its quarry.

Leonard was relieved that he would die held by those he loved. Even so, a tear ran down his left cheek, for this was goodbye, and alas, he wouldn't be able to fulfil his promise that they would see their world change together.

Instead of trying to solve the problem, those crooks had made empty promises and stolen from the people, most of whom had been helplessly indoctrinated into serving their foul masters.

They had implemented their system into schools to pollute the minds of the youth and given paltry sums to their parents to buy their loyalty. People were taught that these vile oppressors were their representatives, their protectors, and their saviours—that society would suffer at the hands of other factions and ideologies. Those swindlers had spun a web so tough that it seemed like nothing would ever cut through it.

So many people had taken their propaganda as truth that even Lev might have believed it, but he had seen the bakeries close, the parks dirtied, the shops boarded up, and the orphanages suffering from disrepair, hardly able to support their children, let alone accept more. He had seen the world he loved disintegrate, and he had realized that this was wrong.

Why are these monsters the only choice? he had thought. *Why do we help the ones who hurt us? Why do we have to aid them, work for them, pay them, and then thank them? Shouldn't they be helping us instead?*

As the years passed, he had worked hard, studied hard, and learned how to lie through his teeth. He had seen those who had tried to fight the autocrats honorably always somehow fall from grace, and disappear. To defeat the monsters, he had to become a monster, but instead of feeding on the weak and downtrodden, he swore to protect them as he devoured their predators. He too had once been a twelve-year-old lad, his life ruined at the greedy hands of the corrupt who'd worsened a devastating recession.

Brutus and Maria had been the first to follow him—since they were practically siblings, it was only natural—and as time went by, others had joined his cause. Two people became four and four became hundreds; his following had grown and grown as he proved himself an enchanting orator.

They had tried to invite him into their ranks like they had many respected professionals before him, but he had refused to submit. Instead, he had foiled their plans and dismantled their traps, and by the time they had realized how much of a threat he was, it had been too late. Their web had been torn apart and the people were awoken.

As a last resort, the tyrants had set loose an assassin to slay their indomitable foe. This was their last chance to pluck this thorn from their sides. The dastards had succeeded.

Lev smiled for the last time and muttered "thank you" as he, much to his friends' grief, closed his eyes.

CHAPTER 1

TRANSMIGRATION

As he closed his eyes, Lev felt nothing—no pain, no fear, no anger, no happiness, and no grief. He felt neither his body nor his mind. He was fading, becoming one with the void. All his hardships were fading, but so were all his dreams. He was to forget his enemies, but was he... to forget his friends?

No! He would not allow it. He would not allow the apathetic emptiness to engulf his mind and steal everything he cared about, everything he had hoped to accomplish, everything he had wished to achieve. He would not let it devour his memories, he would not let it erase his friends and their smiles, and he would not let it destroy what made him *Leonard Erand Vandersteen*!

Lev fought and fought against the ageless, greedy despot who sought to strip him of everything. He fought for what felt like millennia, and finally, the overlord of nothingness conceded. As he felt it release its grip on his awareness, the void around him began to flow, and he lost his bearings.

What's going on? Lev thought as he was swept away at an incredible speed with nothing in his sight but giant orbs of light.

Light? He could see again! But he was more shocked at the wondrous view before him. Orbs of light in myriad colours and patterns darted about. Some swirled to the left, some to the right, upwards, downwards, and some diagonally. There were even orbs dyed in multiple colours that moved in parallel. It was marvellous.

He abruptly felt the current sweep him downwards, and Lev found himself hurtling towards one of the orbs, a green one whose vortex pattern converged in the centre. Panicking, he closed his eyes before briefly losing consciousness.

Upon reawakening, Lev felt a sharp pain on his forehead. *Head?* He could feel his head! Suddenly the pain increased and a loud buzzing sound flooded his ears. He instinctively pressed his hands to his head, touching a soaked rag and detecting a wet sensation on his fingertips.

He opened his eyes to two filthy, grey, spindly arms with five clawed, blood-covered fingers on each hand.

Lev screamed as an onslaught of questions assaulted his already-heavy head. *What's happening? What's going on here! These aren't my hands!*

He looked around and found himself sitting on a filthy hide, in a small filthy room caked in dried blood. A giant brown rag hung over what he assumed was the exit.

As he tried to make sense of his surroundings, a gnarled green hand with yellowish claws pushed the rag to the side, revealing a repulsive bald creature with long ears, a massive, pus-filled, crooked nose, and glowing yellow eyes.

"*Maghag ma gherm*!" croaked a guttural voice in a language alien to his ears.

Lev's headache intensified; it felt like a sledgehammer bludgeoning his brain.

He screamed again. He tried, hand pressed to his forehead, to put distance between himself and the bizarre creature, yet it advanced, screeching in its crude native tongue. When the creature was finally within arm's reach, Lev lost consciousness a second time.

"Wa... Ghe..."

A voice?

"Wak... u... Gher..."

The feminine voice became clearer and clearer.

"Gherm! Wake up, Gherm."

Lev jerked awake to another grey, inhuman figure clad in rags staring down at him. He unwillingly drew air into his chest and prepared to scream once more, only to have a grunt forced from him as he was kicked in the stomach.

"Scream again and I'll kick you harder, got it?" snarled the squinty-eyed creature. Lev nodded breathlessly.

"Good." She sat down on the cot next to him. "So how's your head?"

Gherm? Breath quickening, Lev dropped his face into his hands as waves of new memories deluged his brain, crashing against his old ones. At last the memories settled, leaving Lev out of breath.

"Are you alright?!"

That's right. She's called Ghorza, and she's Gherm's older sister. But I'm not this creature called Gherm! What are these things *even supposed to be, and where did these memories come from?!*

Lev looked at his hands. *These aren't my hands!*

He peeked at his reflection in a bowl of water. *This isn't my face!*

He gazed down at his torso. *This isn't my body!*

"Gherm! Calm down! You're freaking me out!" Ghorza quickly weighed her options. "Should I ask the overseers to get the healer?" she muttered to herself—or so she had hoped, but Lev, or Gherm, had managed to hear it.

Overseers? He winced at the thought of being "healed" by the mad witch doctors of the tribe.

The more time passed, the more he realized how bad his current situation was as his brain accessed more of his newly gained memories. For now, his brain had managed to assimilate about half of them.

From what he understood, these memories belonged to a male specimen of a race called "bogeys" named "Gherm." Bogeys were a goblinoid race whose defining characteristics included physical weakness compared to other races, intelligence superior to that of goblins, natural lifespans averaging sixty years, and the production of fewer offspring than other goblinoids.

Within the bogey race, Gherm and his sister Ghorza had been born into a grey-skinned tribal line known simply as greyborns. As greyborns possessed the greatest magical affinity amongst all bogeykind, they were once a privileged, honoured class. Alas, because of a failed coup by greyborn elitists centuries ago, the entire greyborn tribe had been forbidden from practicing the magical arts, and subsequently their techniques had been lost to time. With every bogey indoctrinated to hate the greyborns for "their" past mistakes, and no magical skills in which the tribe could collectively take pride, it was no wonder that "greyborn" was now synonymous with "worthless trash."

To make matters worse, the bogeys of Lev's tribe were casualties of a war between the Jiira and the Kur. The Jiira, a tribe of goblins, had conquered the greyborns to use their territory as a buffer zone against the Kur, a tribe of kobolds. Now the tribe, especially the greyborns, lived in squalor, mining for a pittance in one of the mysterious magical caverns known to house monsters, magical ores, and treasures created during the age of the gods.

This can't be real... This has to be a nightmare, thought Lev. *It shouldn't be possible for this scenario to happen. It shouldn't be possible for a world like this to exist!* His breath quickened again.

"Gherm! Looks like I really need to ask the overseers."

"No!" Lev blurted out, causing his so-called sister to flinch.

A moment passed in silence. He was thinking about what he should do to prevent this lucid dream from getting worse; she was worried about his repeated outbursts.

Lev took pains to steady his breathing long enough to speak. "I'm okay. It would be disrespectful of us to bother them with such a trivial matter." He feigned a smile.

"But—"

"Just trust me," Lev said a little more forcefully than he had planned. "It's all okay."

"Okay... But please don't scream like that ever again. You'll give me a panic attack! Now get up." Ghorza slung one of his arms over her shoulders. "You've been here long enough, and we're painfully low on merits now."

"Low?"

Slap!

"Ouch!" Lev winced at the stinging pain in his back. "Why'd you slap me *now*?"

"Because you're an idiot!" she cried. "In case you haven't guessed, you were as good as dead when that tunnel collapsed! Thank Vee we had enough merits to save you in the first place!"

Lev sighed. Merits were the closest thing to money that greyborns could readily obtain, and the merits-for-labour system had been spearheaded by the upper class and implemented by the ruling powers to restrict greyborns' access to goods and equipment. With merits, greyborns could buy essentials such as food, water, and clothing, but only of the lowest quality: foodstuffs on the brink of spoilage, water with notes of soap, and tunics sewn out of whatever remnants could be scrounged. Even so, bankruptcy would certainly spell his demise.

That is, if any of this were real.

What a weird dream... I should wake up, or at least turn this one lucid. I'll do a reality check—look at my palm, close my eyes, and then look again.

My palm should be different.

Lev closed his eyes. *Now on 1... 2... 3.* Lev reopened his eyes. His palm was the same.

"No... This can't... be," he mumbled to himself. "Wake up!" he hollered—nothing happened. Lev violently shook his head hoping to shake himself awake—nothing happened. He cracked his knuckles, an old habit, and even pinched himself—nothing happened.

Ghorza felt as if she were in the presence of a madman. "G-Gherm?"

"It's real... This is all real." Tears streamed down his cheeks.

Ghorza slowly approached and gently extended her arm to wrap around him. "Why are you crying? What's wrong? Did something happen—"

"Don't touch me!" Lev snapped, slapping Ghorza's arm away. Lev saw the shock and sorrow in Ghorza's eyes; her younger brother must never have treated her like this before. He suddenly felt his chest tighten, and for once it was not from panic.

"I'm sorry," he began, "I'm really tired right now, and my head is killing me."

"It's alright..."

As Lev stepped out of the room, he immediately found the yellowish-green face from before glaring at him. He scanned Gherm's memories: it was old Rogg, an herbalist who, due to his meagre set of abilities and insolence towards the wrong people, had ended up working here, between the slaves and the poor.

"Have you finally calmed down, you grey wretch?" Rogg hissed. "You just *had* to keep screaming! Do you know *hard* it is to put a gravely injured hunter to sleep using dalk roots without killing him?"

Lev shuddered. The roots of the dalka, a common cave plant, contained a neurotoxin that could easily sedate a goblinoid, but carried a one-in-four chance of putting them to sleep forever. Only a master healer should ever have given Lev dalk roots, and by no measure was Rogg qualified.

Rogg read Lev's face. "Oh, so now even a *slave* thinks he's better than me. If I'd known you were such an ungrateful wretch, I wouldn't have healed you!"

Please. It's not like you did it for free, Lev seethed in his mind. *We all know you checked with the local overseer to see if we had enough merits before Ghorza could get a word in!* Still, as much as he disliked Rogg, Rogg was the only healer in the area who would treat greyborns.

"My apologies, I had never meant to offend such an *esteemed* practitioner of the medical arts." Lev inhaled deeply before delivering his lengthy next line. "*Surely* you can understand that a mere greyborn such as myself never intended to doubt the *greatness* of your skills, let alone insult a *master* healer, such as yourself, who would so much as *deign* to apply his years of scholarship to heal lowly *slaves* like *us*."

From the wide grin on the old man's face, Lev concluded that he had flattered the old coot a little *too* well. It had obviously been a long time since anyone had treated him with respect.

"'*Master* healer'… Alright, You're forgiven this time," he boasted, "but if you look at me like *that* again, death will be the least of your problems!"

"Yes, of course. Thank you for your care, great healer."

"As long as you have the merits, you can come anytime—otherwise, don't waste my time! Now get out. I have other matters to attend to."

Lev and Ghorza obliged with copious thank-yous without protest. Lev was careful not to drop his act until they closed the door behind them.

"What was *that*?" asked Ghorza.

"What was what?"

"That whole act of gratitude and... *submissiveness*. You were kissing his wrinkly old ass more than a priestess of Maga. What happened to you? You've always been a coward, but you've never lowered yourself like *that*."

"Ouch. You don't pull punches, do you?"

"Nope. Never. But you..." Ghorza hesitated. "You *know* that, right?" Something about her brother had changed after waking up, and she did not just mean his "episodes." This Gherm now spoke differently, walked differently, and acted differently. This Gherm was assertive and cunning, completely unlike his old self. It was as if he were no longer her brother.

Was he possessed, or had he lost his memories? Freak accidents like those were rare enough to be legendary, but had certainly happened before. Since Gherm's behavior could also be attributed to aftereffects of the damage or side effects of Rogg's treatment, though, Ghorza decided to give him some time before drawing any conclusions.

They trudged back to their home in the slave quarters near the border of the cavern, far from any clean water source and with only a single-layer wall between them and the monsters of the cavern. Still, it was one of the better parts of the slave quarters.

They had returned home. Now it was time to rest.

CHAPTER 2

MEMORIES OF OLD

"What's wrong?" said Ghorza. "Come on. Eat."

"Not hungry." Lev stared at his dinner. It stared back with six eyes partially hidden behind dull brown fuzz.

Fuzzy cave worms were one of the most abundant species in the magical cavern. Each had two long whiskers stretching from the sides of its head and a long, thin, slippery tongue; the specimen before him, freshly butchered, had its tongue lolling out of its mouth. The worm was half his size, so it was cut into three pieces. Ghorza had served herself the middle part and set aside the bottom for a light breakfast tomorrow. Most pressingly, she had served Lev the head, Gherm's favourite.

"You know, it's pretty expensive to get one of these right now, and you haven't eaten a thing since you woke up. You really don't wanna eat that?"

"Really Ghorza, I'm not—"

Grrrrrrr. His grumbling stomach was loud enough to wake the dead.

"Not hungry, huh?"

Lev was speechless, betrayed by his own body.

"Gherm," Ghorza resumed, holding out a piece of head meat, "eat."

"Maybe it would be—"

"Eat."

"Shouldn't we—"

"*Eat.*"

"It honestly would be better to—"

"*I said eat.*"

"*Fine!*" Truthfully speaking, Lev needed to eat. No matter how disgusted he was at the idea of eating… *bugs*, his survival depended on it, and he had to adapt. Besides, it was not the first time he had been made to eat something questionable.

He grabbed the mud-colored flesh from Ghorza's hand and stuffed it into his mouth without a second thought.

"Gherm? Why are you making that face?" Fuzzy cave worms had been, for as long as she could remember, Gherm's favourite. She had never imagined that she would see him disgusted to eat them.

"N-Nothing to worry about. There was some lazlick mould inside it," he lied, the corners of his lips tensed upwards.

"Oh. Lucky you!" Though Gherm hated the idea of even getting near the mould, Ghorza adored its extremely sweet flavour.

How on earth did Gherm enjoy eating these damned things?" Lev thought. The meat tasted overwhelmingly bitter and sour, and the texture reminded him of vehicle tyres sloshing through a swamp.

Trying his best to maintain a joyful expression, Lev focused entirely on moving his jaws up and down. He finally managed to swallow the worm chunk, hoping the meal was over.

"Now, time to finish the rest," Ghorza sang, relieved her brother was eating again.

His stomach dropped. "Sure," he said, forcing another smile so that he would not gag or cry.

Lev continued feigning joy between bites while making small talk every now and then—Gherm was never the silent type. Every time he talked, he also expressed himself with his hands, and every time Ghorza asked him an embarrassing question, he twitched his ears and nervously tapped on the table with his left index finger. Though their flavor preferences could not be more disparate, Lev was confident that he had replicated all of Gherm's gestures, quirks, and nuances. And to him, at least, it seemed convincing.

Finally, Lev thought as the last bite went down his throat. He stood up, stretched his body, and proceeded to grab a drinking bowl. He then gulped down enough water to wash down the last of the worm meat before handing the bowl to Ghorza.

"Thanks." She took a sip and handed the bowl back to her brother to put away.

"You're welcome."

"Thank the gods you're alright. We're the only family we have left."

"Don't worry, I don't die easily."

"You're saying that as though danger is normal to you. Next you're gonna tell me you're a war hero." Ghorza giggled nervously.

"War hero, huh," he muttered. The room fell silent except for his finger tapping the table as he lost himself in his thoughts.

Ghorza waited, expecting her brother to admit he was joking, but the tapping went on longer than it ever had before. "Gherm. Are you okay?"

Gherm said nothing.

"Gherm?"

Once more, Gherm did not respond.

"*Gherm*!"

Lev nearly dropped the bowl. "So it happened again... Sorry. I was thinking about something."

"I've never seen you like that. Were you really 'thinking about something,' or was it just your injury? Do we need to go back to Rogg?"

"Trust me, it's nothing."

"You do know that you *rarely* lie to me, right? Ever since you woke up, I feel like you've been lying a lot more. Even during dinner, I felt like something was off. Like instead of just *being* yourself, you're trying to *act* like yourself." Ghorza pulled her chair closer to Lev. "Please, Gherm, tell me why, and be honest this time."

Lev was stunned. He was so sure that he could fool her, but something in his mind was urging—no, forcing—him to come clean. The moment his focus lapsed, the influence suddenly took partial control.

"I have memories from another life," Gherm blurted out with wide eyes.

"You're joking."

Lev tried to say yes, but something interfered. "Nope."

"Come on, Gherm, I'm serious."

"So am I."

Ghorza backed away slowly before grabbing a stone knife from the table.

Lev detected that the influence had exhausted itself and was ceding control back to him. He relaxed his eyelids, but it was too late. "Ghorza—"

"So do you only have memories or is it something else?" she demanded. "Are you *really* Gherm?"

The weakened influence tried to take over again, but through sheer force of will, Lev choked out an answer. "Yes. Who else could I be?" he insisted, softly taking a step towards a window.

"Then why are you backing away from me?"

"Because you were always superstitious, and I'm sure you think I'm a demon, even though I'm not."

"Sure you aren't, and I'm the chief's daughter!" She gripped the knife hard enough to turn her knuckles white.

Lev desperately searched Gherm's memories for a way to prove himself to her and found two words that fit. "Meron powder."

"What?" Ghorza gasped.

"Meron powder. I'll mix that meron powder we received in the holy ceremony a year ago with water and drink it. If I start burning..." Lev gulped, "then it'll be obvious I'm possessed and you can do whatever you want with me, but if nothing happens, you'll have to believe that I *am* Gherm, except with memories from another life."

"You're... crazy..."

"I am exactly who I say I am. Just give me a chance to prove myself—you have nothing to lose. In fact, if I am a demon, you'll get your beloved, albeit slightly scorched, brother back. Deal?"

Ghorza hesitated for a second and stepped back far enough to allow Lev to grab the meron powder jar from across the room to the left. She did not lower her knife.

Thank goodness she agreed, thought Lev before hesitantly prying the jar open. *Hopefully the thing about this powder expelling demons and spirits is just superstition, and if it's not, I hope the powder either sends me back to where I belong or at least doesn't hurt.*

He grabbed a pinch of the powder and sighed in relief as nothing happened. He had learned from his earlier rush of knowledge that certain powerful demons could resist the effects from dry powder, but not from powder mixed with water. He stirred the powder into some water, drank the concoction, and braced for impact.

Yet again, nothing happened. Lev's imperceptibly tensed shoulders relaxed completely. "Do you believe me now?"

Ghorza was stunned. "S-So you're really Gherm?"

"No. I'm Tanach, the dreamer of worlds," Lev said sarcastically.

"Pfft! *Tanach!* Out of all your options, you chose the lazy one?"

"What can I say? I love being lazy."

"You sure do, Gherm. You sure do." She paused. "So, care to explain to me how you have other memories?"

With the strange influence from earlier weakened to a suppressible level, Lev was confident that he could lie his way through this, but the method by which he had been reincarnated vaguely resembled something that Gherm's deceased father had mentioned once. *Ghorza might be able to shed some light,* he thought.

"I honestly don't know how it all happened. I felt that I was in a void, and then my body was swept away as if by a river, and then I found myself heading towards a ball of light." While Lev talked, Ghorza's face cycled through a multitude of expressions, among them confusion, shock, excitement, and fear. "After colliding with it—or, rather sinking into it—I woke up with an aching head and an additional set of memories."

Ghorza pulled up a chair and sat at Lev's side. "By the gods, Gherm. Do you realize what this means?"

"No, not at all."

"You're a chosen one. A *chosen one*! It's been a long time since a chosen one appeared, and even longer since a greyborn became one."

"Uh oh." As far as bogeys were concerned, chosen ones were reincarnations of the gods and their godly champions. Chosen ones wielded powers beyond natural potential, ranging from simple augments like superhuman strength to complex capabilities that could alter the very fabric of reality.

"If anyone finds out, you could be killed. Gherm, if you gain any special abilities, never show them to anyone, and never, ever use them unless you absolutely *have* to. Oh, gods, if you needed to use them and someone saw... I don't know what we'd do."

Lev was ready to rattle off a myriad of ways to dispatch whoever saw him, but Ghorza suddenly stood back up. "Maybe you could be lucky and turn out to be a lost soul."

Lost souls were people who had inherited the memories of other mortals. They had new memories, but no new powers whatsoever. Even the new memories were frequently commoners' memories whose antiquity rendered them and their holders entirely unremarkable. Only a few lost souls had ever managed to gain prominence, and even then, they had been fortunate enough to inherit memories from great leaders and legendary craftsmen.

"What do you think? Check your recent memories. Do they contain any divine figures?"

Lev shrugged. "Looks like I'm a lost soul and not a chosen one."

"Thank the gods. I couldn't bear to lose you—"

"Yes, yes, thankfully it's just a commoner's memory," dismissed Lev self-assuredly. "But not the kind of commoner that you're thinking of. Not even one from this world." Lev knew bogeys told folk tales involving both transmigration and latent memories. As far as Gherm's memories served him, though, no one, not even in folklore, had ever inherited memories from another world, and no one had ever lost control of their body to the foreign consciousness instead of integrating.

Lev postulated that in his case, either there had been a problem in the reincarnation process, or his resistance to his own world's reincarnation process had triggered a failsafe that had sent him into this world. There was also the possibility that supernatural entities were meddling with current events.

"Great!" Ghorza restarted. "But you should still keep quiet. Who knows what secrets lie in your new memories?" Ghorza rubbed her forehead, trying to relax her long-furrowed brow.

"That's why I didn't want to tell you. I *know* my status isn't something I can disclose easily. I *know* that if others find out, I could be hunted down, tortured, and killed. I *know* lost souls are still rare, so if I do get caught, I could be cut open and experimented on by mages and researchers hoping to discover my hidden gifts, or maybe just to amuse themselves while they flaunt their superiority over me as they probe me both physically and mentally and laugh as they twist me and break me while stripping me of—"

"*Stop!*" Ghorza shrieked with a fury she had never shown even when she had thought Lev was a demon. "*Never* say anything like that again! Never... please..." Her voice faltered as she embraced her brother.

Lev felt tears wet his shoulder and realized that he had taken it too far. His chest tightened; he knew he was frequently guilty of verbalizing the worst-case scenario without considering how it would affect others.

And due to what could only be Gherm's influence, he felt particularly guilty. Lev hugged her back and let Ghorza cry on his shoulder, and when she had calmed down, he smiled at her. "Let's go to sleep now and leave the thinking for tomorrow."

"Yeah, sleep, let's go to sleep." Ghorza lingered in her brother's embrace for a moment before they both released each other. "We've got a lot of work to do tomorrow to earn back those merits."

After cleaning the dining room and storing the remaining worm meat, "Gherm" and Ghorza retired to their sleeping quarters and lay on their separate mats, which were made from old rags bought with hard-earned merits.

"Good night, Gherm," said Ghorza before she closed her eyes and entered the land of dreams.

"Good night," Lev replied before closing his eyes. He waited a few minutes until the rhythm of Ghorza's breathing slowed before breaking his façade and losing himself once again in his thoughts.

So I died, huh, Lev deduced. He recalled what had happened at the moment of his death. He had been shot during his victory speech, and Brutus and Maria had come to his aid.

Heh... I'm pretty sure the big lug cried like a baby. Despite his large, intimidating physique, he was always a big softie. Maria, on the other hand, now she *was a tigress,"* Lev thought as he remembered how she'd always gotten into street fights no matter the odds.

He reminisced about their childhood as a tear fell from his eye. *Will I ever see them again? My life loses a bit of its meaning without them.* Lev felt Gherm sympathising with him; he scowled at the subhuman beast whose body he had been made to share.

Sorry, Gherm, but from what I've seen and from what I've known from your memories, you'll be trouble in the future. I'm not the type to kill innocents, but I'll try putting you to sleep for now. He did not know how to influence souls, and before today he had doubted their existence, but in his experience, he had managed to regain control over his body purely due to his greater willpower.

Lev tried focusing his will to silence Gherm. Earlier, he had overpowered Gherm's soul enough to control his body, but despite his efforts now, he couldn't even dampen Gherm's influence on his emotions.

Well, that's that. I'll deal with you once I figure out how to. And trust me, I always figure things out. He felt Gherm brush his warning off.

Fine. Yes. We're stuck in the same body, and by this I mean your life sucks, Lev acquiesced. *But who said I'll settle for the same life you did? Do you think I'm content with that?* he quizzed while scrutinizing his hands. Gherm's life had been anything but easy. The abuse of greyborn was the norm, and though some non-greyborn bogeys tried to act civilized and merciful by selling items to them, greyborns still paid more for goods that were all too often of the worst quality. Even small-time criminals, as long as they did not have grey skin, were treated better.

I need to find a way to improve my life, and I need to take care of her, Lev thought as he looked at the sleeping Ghorza. Even though he was not exactly Gherm, he had still inherited Gherm's memories, so he knew how much Gherm cared about his sister. He realized that considering how easily he had come to accept his change in environment, he might be merging with Gherm, a prospect that, he perceived, horrified Gherm. Thankfully, because of Lev's superior strength of will, their fusion would be more of Gherm assimilating into Lev rather than Lev taking on any of Gherm's negative traits.

Many questions swirled in Lev's head, but he knew he would not be able to answer them all in a single night. Closing his eyes, he allowed himself to drift off to sleep.

CHAPTER 3
TWO-FACEDNESS

"Ugggh," groaned Lev, his eyes closed and his chest aching. He tried to get up; the force of two gentle hands stopped him.

"Whoa there, buddy. Don't move too much. You've taken a shot to the chest and you're still in critical condition."

Lev was shocked as he heard a voice he thought he would never hear again.

"Brutus?" asked Lev as he turned to his left.

"The one and only."

"So it was just a dream. Thank God."

"What did you dream about?" asked a woman's voice Lev had missed just as much coming from the other side of his hospital bed.

As Lev turned to face Maria, he briefly surveyed his surroundings, a perfectly unremarkable hospital room with white walls and a grey floor, filled with the beeping of machines and the smell of disinfectant, most unremarkably with nary a trace of goblin.

"Haha! You won't believe how crazy it was. I was stuck in a void for a long time. Then I got turned into some kind of a slave. I wasn't even human. Imagine that!" He gazed at his hands, each with five perfectly unremarkable fingers, and clenched them tightly.

"That really does sound crazy," Brutus chuckled, shaking his head.

"I know! Anyways, both of you, give me a hand. I need to get out of bed and back on the Council right away." Lev reached one hand out to Brutus and one hand out to Maria, grateful for their unwavering support. "Considering that *their* sabotage has failed, we can use this to our advan… tage…"

Lev froze as his gaze drifted down from Maria's face to his outstretched hand. To his surprise, he saw seven spindly, pale fingers.

"How disappointing. This is a dream, isn't it?"

"I'm sorry, man. There's nothing we can do," said Brutus, his voice starting to muddy and echo.

"I miss you both."

"You know we miss you too," replied Maria, whose face became blurrier and blurrier as she spoke. "But it's time to wake up, Lev. Promise us that you'll make the best of your new life and never give up,"

"I do. You can count on that," Lev answered without hesitation.

"Great! We hope you'll change the world for the better," whispered the duo in unison as the room began to fall away starting at the edges of Lev's vision.

"Is that supposed to be a question? You two of all people should know that I'm gonna shake this world's foundations to its very core. Just… Please try to visit me as much as you can."

Lev heard Brutus' booming voice echo across the growing distance between Lev and what remained of his hotel room. "We will. For now, he will keep you company." Brutus pointed at a small, translucent, grey figure Lev had not noticed all along.

"Gherm. Got anything else? Anything better and less annoying?"

"Hey!" yapped Gherm.

"Nope." Maria's soft murmur comfortingly caressed Lev's ears.

"Oh, come on! I have feelings, too, you know!"

Brutus was about to tease the grey bogey, but his piece, too, fell away.

"Guess our time is up. It's time to wake up, Lev."

It's time to wake up, Lev.

It's time to wake up, Gherm.

"I said it's time to wake up, Gherm! We've got a lot of work to do today!" yelled the older sister.

He opened his eyes to the girl who was about to kick him awake.

"Looks like you're pretty hyper this early in the morning."

"Well, one of us has to be," admonished Ghorza. "Is it that hard for you to wake up early by yourself?"

Lev sat up and stretched contentedly. "I'll try and make it a habit. Are you ready for breakfast?" he told her with a confident smile, something Gherm would never have done.

"So it did change you. Please don't change anymore..." Her voice trailed off, and for a moment, neither of them could find the words to say.

"Let's go eat, shall we?" Lev had no more time for tension.

They reheated the remainder of the previous night's meal and ate it as fast as they could. As they ate, Ghorza glanced at Lev. His posture was more confident and his eating habits were more refined than she had ever seen.

"Are you sure you didn't inherit the memories of a noble?" Ghorza asked, her mouth full of bug meat.

Lev swallowed. "Yup."

"You sure are acting like one, minus the condescending attitude."

"Well, the memories came from a different life in a different society. The owner of these memories tried to make his society a better place, only to get assassinated by his noble rivals."

"You're not going to try to overthrow the rule of the blues, right?" spoke Ghorza hurriedly, who almost choked on the food filling her mouth.

Lev stared at her as if she were the village fool. "How dumb do you think I am?"

"Well..."

"Sure, sure. Fight them head-on! Just let me go grab my armour and spear while you go call my loyal armies and mages to fight not only the rest of our kind but also our lovely goblin overlords. Oh wait, I'm not a warrior with weapons and armour, and I command neither armies nor mages."

"Mages?" asked the dumbfounded girl. She hadn't expected her brother to talk to her like that.

"Magic users like shamans, only less spiritual and more methodical."

"Oh, I get it—wait, does that mean you know magic?!" The idea of her brother knowing magic gave her as much fright as the idea of overthrowing the chiefdom, for greyborns were forbidden from practising magic.

"No. And can you please stop jumping to wild conclusions like that? If I knew magic, wouldn't you feel me practicing it?" asked Lev, getting more annoyed every time Ghorza said something that would end with him having a slashed throat, a noose around his neck or his decapitated head on a stick.

Speaking of "feeling" magic, though greyborns had forgotten the arts, they retained the ability to sense magical energy and could detect magical residue when the arts were used. Because of their ability to detect magic combined with their expendability, goblins had sent many a greyborn to scout the lower levels ahead of their expedition parties.

Ghorza grinned and nodded at her now-different younger brother. She didn't fully believe him, but she chose to give him the benefit of the doubt.

They continued eating their meal in silence, each lost in their own thoughts. Lev was brainstorming what he would do to climb the ladder of bogey society out of the greyborn caste. It was rare, but not impossible: greyborns who had climbed the ladder before him had performed miraculous feats to be conferred normal commoner status.

Ghorza fret over fast her brother changed after becoming a lost soul. *Would he one day become a different person?* Usually, the inheritor of the memories would change a little, but not this much. Would her greatest fear come true? Would he not be her brother anymore?

After finishing their meal, Lev got to his feet. "And done. Now let's go already."

"You're awfully quick today. Usually you'd take your time to avoid arriving early."

Lev shrugged. "Well, we burned a lot of merits treating me, right?"

"True. Things will be tough on us for a while"

"*If* you work on your own, that is. But don't worry. I'll work extra hard to cover the costs."

"You? Work *hard*? Yeah, right!" Ghorza laughed. Gherm had always earned half the amount of merits she did.

"You shouldn't treat it as a joke. Trust me on this. After today, I'll no longer have problems earning merits," he told her, satisfied with himself and his plan to get rid of *the* problem once and for all.

"Sure you will."

"You'll see. Now let's get ready."

After they ate, got dressed, and grabbed their equipment, they left the house and walked to the work quarters to receive their assignments from the taskmaster.

As they walked, Lev checked his surroundings to fill any discrepancies in his memory, as well as to familiarize himself with Gherm's memories. He and his sister were situated in the southwestern quarters where housing ranged from dilapidated shacks, where the most pitiful slaves lived, to the humble huts of those better off. Gherm's abode probably fell in the middle.

"What a surprise. I thought you'd croaked," said the taskmaster to Lev with a grin as they arrived.

"Not this time, Kul. And I won't die anytime soon if I can help it," replied Lev to the old pale green bogey. Kul had once been an honoured member of the warrior class—he had been considered one of the best and had mentored many elites—but after failing to protect a noble's son during the war with the Jiira, he was forced to step down and ended up a taskmaster in the slave quarters.

Through the years, he'd learned to let go of his prejudice and had managed to overcome the indignation of his downfall. He still hated the upper class for this humiliation, but unlike the other taskmasters, he never took his anger out on the slaves. As he treated his workers as individuals, many greyborn respected and even liked him.

"Are you sure you're ready to continue working?" asked Kul. "I can transfer some of my merits to you if you can't." Gherm's father, Gat, had been the first to befriend Kul and had helped him see the greyborn as individuals. Any time Kul had trouble with a slave, as long as the task was reasonable, Gat would persuade that slave to cooperate. Kul owed him a lot and since Gat and his wife had both been killed when a swarm of lesser hivelings raided the village two years ago, Kul had never gotten the chance to adequately express his gratitude, so he tried to help Gat's children instead.

"Don't worry about me, Kul. I'm feeling much better."

"That's right, gramps. He's as fit as he can be," Ghorza added.

"'Gramps'? Who're you calling '*gramps*'? I can still beat your ass and everyone else's with one hand tied behind my back!" yelled the miffed Kul, causing everyone in the nearby vicinity to awkwardly laugh while slowly giving him some space. Though he meant it as a joke, they all knew that he was telling the truth.

"Sorry," Ghorza said while lowering her head.

Kul tried to maintain his angry expression, but he failed and burst out laughing.

"I know you didn't mean any harm, lass. But make sure to not piss off the wrong people," he said with a gentle smile.

"I know that. I'm not an idiot. But I can still beat up anyone who pisses us off, right?"

"As long as they're fellow greyborns, no offence."

"None taken," Ghorza replied nonchalantly. She realized the consequences of what would happen if a greyborn harmed a non-greyborn, even if they were a fellow slave. She was not even that interested in fighting others, but showing weakness usually led to exploitation, so she had to act tough.

After finishing their talk, it was time to get to work, so Kul took on a professional visage and assigned the brother and sister their tasks.

"Good luck, little bro. Make sure to avoid any trouble," said Ghorza before they separated and went to their respective stations. Ghorza to the mushroom farms, Lev to the mining quarters.

Dear sister, trouble will come as always, Lev thought, *except this time will be the last time it ever bothers us.* He approached the mining area for two purposes: first and foremost, to continue to earn merits, and second, to not only finish his job, but also deal with one of the main hurdles of his life: a hurdle by the name of Rak.

CHAPTER 4

FRIENDS AND FOES

It was supposed to be a regular day of work for Rak.

Today, like most days, his group was assigned to mining duty, one of his favourite pastimes. It was easier to extort weaker slaves in the mining quarters where there were no guards; no guard would risk dying in a cave to watch a bunch of slaves.

Rak knew the issues of his lifestyle. He knew that one day he would cross the wrong person. But he couldn't stop himself—not anymore.

He closed his yellow-pupiled eyes and reminisced about how it had come to this.

* * *

Throughout his entire life, he had been reputed to be strong. He had always been stronger than almost all the other bogeys, and he was as strong as, if not stronger than, the average goblin. Despite his physical advantage, though, he never would have used it to abuse or rule over his peers. At least, so it had been until just a few years ago.

Rak's mother occupied a special place in his heart—not just for having birthed him, but also for having chosen to not abandon him or his two siblings after their father died protecting them from a group of deranged thugs. Rak had seen too many parents abandon or kill their infants during hard times.

She had even sacrificed her dignity by selling her body whenever her children were sick and she didn't have enough merits to send them to a healer. She had always showed them love and compassion and never blamed them or mistreated them even though she could've lived a better life if she'd never had them or at least only had a single child. She had taught him to hold back his fists and only fight whenever it was necessary. To not get into pointless fights driven by arrogance or faulty pride, and to ignore whatever insults others hurled at him, her, his father, or siblings. After all, words were only words and should never result in violence unless taken to the extreme.

One day, his strong mother had fallen gravely ill. When Rak and his siblings had discovered her, she was on the ground fading in and out of consciousness, with blackish green spots covering what could be seen of her grey skin. While his siblings had frantically tried to comfort her and keep her awake, Rak had run to get a healer, but their service was too costly for a band of children to pay. To save their mother, Rak and his siblings had asked their neighbours and friends for help.

"You want us to help that whore? It's her fault for selling her body and angering the gods!"

"I appreciate everything you and your mother have done for us, but if I help her, people will think I'm cheating on my wife, and I don't want that kind of reputation... so I'm sorry, but please go away..."

"We might also be slaves, but we don't want to be lumped together with the likes of your mother!"

"She was just a fling! I'm married now and I don't want my wife to think I'm involved with that harlot, so leave!"

The more he remembered the refusals of those from whom he had requested aid, the more he bristled. The more he remembered the disapproving faces of those who had denounced the value of his mother's labour, the more he gnashed his teeth.

"Bo—"

His mother had always taught him to treat others with kindness, and she embodied that lesson—yet when they had needed help, they had been abandoned as if they were garbage!

"Boss—"

And as her condition had worsened, every single client of hers, for whose livelihoods she had kept quiet and stealthy, had publicly denounced her, claiming "it was what she deserved."

"H-He— Let— go—"

"She did so much for those ingrates—met them late at night, listened to their problems, offered advice where she could—and for what! All because of their stupid prejudices, we became unworthy of help! When she wasn't of use to them anymore and became unable to fend for herself, *they* showed their true nature and treated us like trash! If only I could grab each and every one of them by the throat and choke the living hell out of them, I'd... hmm?"

Suddenly Rak felt pain in his arm, waking him from his moment of recollection, only to find himself choking Hem with that same arm. "Boss— please— let me— go—"

Rak immediately let go of Hem.

Hem coughed for a few seconds while lying on the floor. As he got up, he replied, "Dammit Rak, it's been the third time already this week. If you don't get a hold of yourself, more people will leave the gang and join Vyrga's."

Rak snarled at the name like a beast. After his mother's death, he had resorted to extortion to feed his siblings. Due to his immense strength, he had eventually formed a gang with others in similar circumstances. Even though they were a bunch of criminals, they were one of the cleaner gangs as Rak still maintained some of his standards. They mostly stole, imposed protection fees on whoever they could, and bullied those Rak thought deserving. Still, they stayed far away from the shadier stuff.

Unlike Rak, Vyrga had no such reluctances. Though Vyrga was less concerned with physical strength, his gang was definitely wealthier—

whatever victims they trafficked, researchers seeking "test subjects" and nobles with certain *perversions* were all too happy to buy.

Rak took a deep breath and cleared his thoughts. "This had better be important. Out with it."

Hem scratched his head in embarrassment. "Actually, it's nothing. I just wanted to tell you that a certain bug just came back to work." Hem gestured at the "bug."

Rak narrowed his eyes. "Gherm."

He once again sank back into his memories to remind himself of why he hated folk like Gherm.

In the beginning, when he had started his gang, Rak had still held on to some of his ideals, and had protected those who not only fell under the same circumstances as him and the other members of his gang, but were too weak to fend for themselves.

Rak had first met Veit when they were both children. Veit's mother had abandoned him when his father had died, leaving Veit to fend for himself against older, bigger, and stronger bogey-children who saw no problem taking food from him, at least until Rak had shown up.

As adults, Veit and Rak had been nearly complete opposites. While Rak had been the tallest, most imposing goblinoid most of his cave-dwelling compatriots had ever encountered, Veit had remained small enough to be mistaken for a child. While Rak had been brave and stalwart, Veit had been timid and non-confrontational. After Rak had saved him, Veit had decided to follow Rak around, and the two became almost inseparable despite their differences. Rak valued Veit as a brother who would never betray him.

Every year, an expedition squad consisting of both bogeys and goblins commenced in order to conquer and explore the lower levels of the cavern. The squads were arranged in a loose formation made mostly of bogeys. The most "expendable" members of society were placed on the outer regions of the formation, covering the front, sides, and flank while those higher up were positioned more safely in the inside of the formation.

The objective of this loose formation was to guard the few goblins in the centre from monsters, traps, and other threats. During the last expedition a year ago, Rak and Veit had been chosen to serve in the vanguard along with Vyrga and a few of his men. The vanguard was the thickest line, mostly consisting of untrained grunts. Their purpose was to sacrifice themselves in order for the higher ranks to reach their destination; in return, in most cases, they received merits with the amount varying depending on the achievements of the grunt or grunts who performed said actions.

That expedition had lasted three months, which was on the long end of usual. Vyrga's reputation had preceded him, so Rak had kept his guard up throughout the journey. The last thing he and his best friend had needed was to be dragged into violence by the impulses of an ambitious, amoral greyborn.

But Rak had never expected who that greyborn would be.

The expedition party had reached the sixth floor, and half the greyborn membership had been ordered to scout ahead of the group to sniff out any beast packs or hiveling nests in the nearby vicinity. Based on information from the last expedition that had reached the sixth floor four years ago, the sixth floor was one of the strangest and most populated floors, housing an underground forest with a glowing sphere of bluish-white light in the ceiling. According to the shamans, the sphere was a giant mana crystal that gave light, and life, to the forest.

The scouting group had moved as a single party, every member maintaining a watchful gaze upon the others, until they had reached a key landmark: a giant tree embedded with the fossilized remains of various underground species. There, they had further separated into four smaller groups: one led by Rak, one led by Rak's follower Olf, one by Vyrga, and one more by a warrior known as Mirgar.

Since Rak had been assigned the most dangerous region, Veit had requested to stay with Olf. Rak had agreed, and the groups had gone their separate ways.

A few hours later, it had come time to meet back at the tree. On the way back, Rak had found Olf bloodied on the ground. In a panic, he had ordered his subordinates to stay on guard as they investigated the situation. Olf's throat had been slit; his face was frozen into a shocked expression. His body was mangled beyond recognition.

Rak had roared in anger at the death of his compatriot as his face contorted into a mask of fury. But before long, his anger had transformed into fear, for Veit. He had searched the surroundings for clues and found the bloody footsteps of Olf's murderer.

Rak's squad had chased after them, despite knowing full well that it was a trap, to find Veit lying on his stomach near some trees. Despite all the dangers, Rak had rushed to his friend's side, only to duck and narrowly miss a few javelins that had been aimed at his torso.

Vyrga and his thugs had launched their attack, but thankfully Rak's band had been prepared for any traps, so they had been able to hold back the attackers.

Bogeys from both sides were out for blood, ready to defeat their rivals once and for all. They had charged at each other with stone-tipped spears and flint knives, for under Jiira rule, bogeys were not allowed to even wield copper, let alone bronze, weaponry.

For a few short moments, the two sides had clashed. Spears had been thrust and blades had been stabbed at their enemies. Cries of pain had echoed in the forest as its ground filled with bodies, of both the injured and dead.

In the beginning, it had seemed that Vyrga would be victorious, as not only had his ambush been a success, but he had also brought along twice as many men for the battle. But, he had forgotten that quantity didn't always win over quality.

Vyrga's men were weak, undisciplined and cowardly, unlike Rak's. Rak had never neglected to establish order and discipline among his ranks, and had always made sure that his men continued their combat training, as he knew that they would need to be strong to protect their people from the greedy claws of their rivals.

Vyrga had realized that if things continued the way they had been, he would lose, so he had decided to join the battlefield and strike at the enemy's leader, Rak. He had signalled for three of his elites to join him and they had charged towards their target.

Rak had held his stone axe high and prepared his stance to receive the attack but suddenly, to his surprise, Vyrga had whistled just when he was halfway across.

This had confused Rak—why would his opponent suddenly whistle?—until he had felt a sharp pain in the back of his chest.

He had looked back. Veit had been holding a bloody copper dagger with a rueful smile.

"Boss!" The majority of Rak's men had screamed after witnessing their leader bleeding.

"Stand down if you value his life!" Vyrga had shouted as he and his minions surrounded their enemy's wounded leader.

"Why?" Rak had asked—the question that then dominated his thoughts above all else. He had felt his movements slow—the dagger had been poisoned. How could Veit have betrayed him for something as trivial as merits? But as Rak had heard the words he never wanted to hear, he had understood how wrong about Veit's nature he had been.

"Sorry, Rak. Being friends was nice and all, but being friends with you alone could never ensure me a good life. A connection with the nobles on the other hand? That definitely *will*! I'll be sure to tell your sister how you died valiantly saving the expedition from a hiveling swarm, and maybe after I give her a shoulder to cry on," Veit gestured obscenely, "she'll feel... *grateful*, you know? Hahahaha!"

Veit's expression soured. "I always envied how you had everything going right for you. You have power, loyal men, and a sister with *such* a lovely body! But I realized," he gabbed, "you also lacked something called *awareness*. Anyway, thank you for everything, you were a good friend and I'll cherish everything you'll leave behind."

"Heh...Hehehe..." Rak had giggled menacingly.

Vyrga, apprehensive, had backed away. "Why's he giggling like an idiot and not dead?" he scolded Veit. "Do you know how hard it was to convince a few of my acquaintances to slip me a good copper dagger? You should've finished the job instead of saying your goodbyes!" It was never a good sign when an injured bogey giggled.

"I thought you'd prefer the honour of delivering the killing blow, my lord," Veit had replied in a humble voice.

"'Lord,' huh? Lord Vyrga the Great... Sounds nice. But it would be better for you to finish him. 'A mighty warrior dies at the hands of his traitorous friend' sounds poetic, wouldn't you agree?" Vyrga had stood behind his three elites. His instincts had screamed at him to run away, but he had only had one chance to get rid of this threat, so he had chosen to leave it to the backstabbing wretch.

A moment had passed in silence before Veit conceded. "As you wish."

"Stop, you bastard!" one of Rak's loyal men had cried out. "Men, attack!" They charged in from all directions in a last-ditch effort to free their leader. Vyrga's men had been too distracted to respond quickly.

Veit had held the dagger high with both hands, looking like a cultist performing a sacrifice, ready to strike at his former boss and friend, only to lose feeling in his hands. He had looked up to find his hands were gone.

"ARRGHH!" he had howled in pain before also losing his legs and howling even more. His torso had hit the ground with a loud thud, yet despite the sensory overload from which he was suffering, he had not passed out from shock and was trying to understand what had happened. Veit had looked skyward, and locked eyes with a large figure, consumed by rage and disgust, holding a bloody axe—Rak.

"I'll deal with you later," Rak had said in the darkest tone Veit had ever heard in his life.

Vyrga's elites had panicked and looked backwards to their boss for direction, only to find that he had disappeared.

The demoralized henchmen had no longer posed much of a threat, and the maddened Rak had butchered them one by one while his men dealt with the rest.

In the end, Vyrga's ambush had failed and he had lost a third of his men, while Rak had lost half of his, with half of the remaining men suffering from varying degrees of injuries. Thankfully, not many had been serious.

"Rak... buddy... Please... spare me... I was forced into this. They would've killed everyone I care about if I refused," the foul traitor had begged for mercy.

"So they would have killed you. You've never cared about anyone else and even if I let you live, you never will."

Rak had grabbed Veit and placed him roughly on his shoulder before heading west.

"Wh-Where are we going? The camp's in the east."

"We're not going to the camp," said Rak, trailed by his remaining squad.

"Where else will we go? There's nothing this way except... no... it can't be! Anything but that!"

"Here we are," Rak had said, standing a good distance away from a hivelings' nest.

"I beg you! Don't do it! Don't kill me like this! *Nooo!*" Veit had shrieked as Rak flung him at the nest.

"Ooof!" Veit had grunted as he hit the ground. He had tried to locate an escape but had only made eye contact with a hiveling eagerly poking out from one of the holes in the nest.

"Rak! Help! I'm sorry!" Veit had spluttered as hundreds of hivelings emerged and swarmed towards him.

The agonized screams of Veit were the last thing that Rak had heard as he and his underlings returned to the expedition team.

After that expedition had ended, Rak had purged his ranks of weaklings and potential turncoats, and he had abandoned those pointless ideals that held him back. He and Vyrga became sworn enemies, but only secretly so as not to be manipulated by other factions. Still, they had had some skirmishes and constantly tested each other's territory by harassing the other party's weaker members.

"Boss. Look who decided to play in our zone," said Hem, waking Rak from his flashback. A few of Vyrga's goons were approaching a couple of weaklings who were cowering in fear.

Rak shook his head. Vyrga's trash never seemed to learn that the mining quarters was his territory. Rak moved to intervene, but something he had once thought unimaginable happened before his very eyes.

Gherm inserted himself between Vyrga's men and their target.

CHAPTER 5

BEAUTIFUL WORLD

WARNING: you have 10% charge left in your MCS.

Huh. How did I end up in this ditch?

Lev's fingers moved towards his MCS display screen, blue light reflecting off his visor.

The MCS display had a few tabs and two large blue buttons, conveniently labelled "Alert" and "Close." Lev must have forgotten to stop the automatic alert notification system, which now was screaming at him to recharge his batteries.

Now, where exactly am I? Lev thought as he rolled onto his belly and propped himself up on his arms. *I've got to make contact with the command centre or I'll—*

Lev was rudely interrupted by a deafening explosion a few meters away from him.

Must have been a mortar shell, Lev concluded; mortar shells had to land near their targets to kill, and since his headgear had protected his eardrums while his combat suit had shielded him from shrapnel, he had been spared from any real harm.

Thus was the benefit of having an MCS, short for Military Combat Suit. This was not the official name of the suit, but many cadets simplified it for convenience's sake instead of repeating the long and tedious "Mechanized Military Personal Combat Protection Gear."

"Aargh!" Lev felt a burning pain in his lower torso. He reached down to examine his body for wounds, and found that a bullet had pierced his suit.

When did I get shot? He couldn't remember much—he only knew that staring at empty dirt impact craters would do him no favours.

Right, I need to contact HQ and get the hell out of here.

Lev opened another display, this time on his right wrist. It was an old-fashioned display, one that required him to look down at it instead of beaming its information to his visor. He opened a few sub-tabs.

Confirm your ID.

Lev took out his dog tag and tapped it against his wrist display.

ID Confirmed. Executing action: Contact HQ.

While the device tried to establish a connection, Lev continued walking.

Lev crossed the hill, bristling at the countless bodies—no, body parts—and wrecked vehicles scattered everywhere he could see. Empty shells littered the ground; the smell of gunpowder and discharged plasma rounds still wafted in the air.

Lev's world was embroiled in war—in a worldwide war of untold scale unprecedented in the annals of history. This was not a war about ideology, politics, or anything of the abstract sort; this was simply a war over territory. Both the Technocracy and the Empire needed command over the neutral zone, a zone with "plenty of resources and fertile land," or so the propaganda said.

Lev heard a familiar beep. His wrist device had managed to contact HQ, and a transport vehicle was on its way to his location.

After a brief moment passed, Lev heard another familiar noise, the din of atmospheric thrust engines, the same engines that had dropped him on the battlefield so many times before.

The transport vehicle landed near Lev on flat terrain, heedlessly crushing corpses and debris beneath it. A man walked out of the transport's cargo hatch.

"Recruit Lev, are you enjoying the view? Get on—we haven't got all day!"

* * *

Huh. Time flies, thought Lev. That rescue operation had occurred during Lev's first year of his military service; today marked the conclusion of Lev's tenth year in the United Technocracy of Eurasia's army.

From what Lev had been taught, major economic collapse, precipitated by mismanagement of natural resources, had sent many countries, both developed and developing, into inescapable debt. To recover from the crisis, the United Technocracy of Eurasia and the other major international powers had begun a military campaign to subjugate all weaker nations that still had healthy stocks of natural reserves. For that reason, Eurasia had begun an aggressive recruiting programme: serve in the army for a full ten years, and you would be granted full citizenship in Eurasia, which meant that the Eurasian government would assume all your debts.

Citizenship also conferred the right to civic engagement: you would be able to vote, run for public office, and possibly be elected to the United Council. Most strikingly, even if only one person from an entire family served ten years, all their relatives would be conferred full citizenship and all the benefits and opportunities that followed.

Per what he had been told of his medical records, Lev had been born in the slums almost twenty-three years ago. When he had left to join the army, he had known he had no choice—living in ignorance and squalor was a life neither for him nor the ones he loved. With full citizenship, he would be eligible for meritocratic election to the United Council and hopefully secure a better future for everyone. Lev believed he could change the world.

* * *

Lev quickly brushed the inner parts of his MCR-17 combat rifle, then filled his magazines with another round of plasma discharge capsules. This was his first day in Zone-10, formerly known as England. He had never been stationed in such a peaceful place before; all he knew were the harsh battles he had had to endure in the neutral zone and the less-than-comfortable stations at its borders.

"ALRIGHT MAGGOTS, TIME FOR ANOTHER ROUND OF TRAINING!" barked the sergeant.

Lev knew he would never be promoted to a higher rank in the military; only people with limited citizenship could entertain that idea. Limited citizenship was the beauty of the levy system—if you failed to complete your ten years but had managed to survive at least five, you would receive limited citizenship. If you served the remainder of your original ten years plus an additional ten-year stretch, the Technocracy would deem you worthy of full citizenship. The fastest way to full citizenship, of course, would be to grit one's teeth and endure ten years in a single stretch.

Many saw the levy system as a trap. Limited citizenship would entice people to enlist and quit after five years, but the moment the poverty and helplessness of life as a "limited" citizen set in, those same people would enlist for another ten years.

"THAT MEANS YOU TOO, LEV!"

Private Leonard Erand Vandersteen, tenth year, Eurasian Army was ready for another training session.

Lev stood up and followed the others. Lev could very well have been the most experienced soldier in this base, even more experienced than the sergeant who left for limited citizenship.

First up was the standard eight-kilometer full-gear run. Lev had prepared himself for this session, his muscles ready for more.

"Corporal. This Lev... How long has he been in the army?" Mark asked his second in command. Mark was Lev's platoon sergeant and another victim of the limited citizenship system.

"Well, at least three years longer than you, Sergeant," Eric answered back. Eric was a corporal with a similar story—after having served five years, he had quit to recuperate from the various physical and mental traumas combat had caused. He had then returned to the battlefield, ready for an additional ten years in hell. "This guy's been here for nine years, according to these records. He always survives battles with his magazines empty and his combat suit a wreck."

"So that explains his stamina." Mark shook his head sorrowfully. "He must've been outmanoeuvring those mortar shells for years."

"Damn those Imperials. If only they'd accepted Higman's proposal back in the day, we wouldn't even have had this war to begin with," bemoaned Eric. Councillor Arnold Higman had proposed measures to unify all of Earth under one state. In his most famous speech, he'd started off with these famous words: "For peace to reign, we must unite the world."

Arnold Higman had been assassinated exactly ten milliseconds after those famous last words.

"Corporal. Higman was a delusional old geezer who wanted to be dictator power over the entire world." Mark had wanted to believe that a world like that was possible, but his faith had run out a long time ago. Now, he was just a drone carrying out orders from above. "TIME FOR SIT-UPS, MAGGOTS!" boomed Mark.

Lev and the other recruits did what Mark ordered, most with loud complaints, Lev without.

"Hah, these pansies must be fresh from their mamas' gardens," Eric jeered.

Mark almost played along, but Lev was still going, doing yet more sit-ups with unwaveringly perfect form. *That Lev, he's something different. Are all nine-year term recruits like that?* Mark had never seen a recruit serve all ten years in one stretch, ignoring the promises of limited citizenship and going straight for full.

Another week passed, and the new recruits had been deemed ready for their first battle. Every recruit was assigned a combat suit programmed to execute complex battle movements and increase their odds of survival, though durability and features depended on rank. Sadly, only the very basics were explained to the recruits, and it would take at least a month for trash from the slums to be moulded into combat-ready soldiers.

Lev heard that familiar sound that had been ever present throughout the past nine years, and before he knew it, there it stood: the dreaded combat assault vehicle, atmospheric engines spouting out huge amounts of compressed air.

"Alright, men! Check your combat suits before entering and hang on tight!" Mark shouted at the cadets, knowing that less than half of them would survive this first battle.

"And don't forget, lads, a fresh pint for the lucky one who gets the most kills!" bellowed Eric. The innocent recruits took Eric's joke seriously, laughing about how they would tell their grandchildren about the "Great War."

Lev did not join in; he was preoccupied with checking all of his equipment one last time. He knew he would just see the battlefield tear their legs off and splatter their brains next to their broken skulls. He saw no reason to socialize.

He stepped into the vehicle, securing himself and his suit to the support rack.

"Remember to release your suits when the light turns green!"

"Aye-aye, sir!"

Lev inadvertently made eye contact with Mark, snapping himself out of his daze. "Aye-aye, sir!" he replied hastily.

This was it, the transport to hell. Lev had long since lost count of how many battles he had fought, but he knew that every single one had had the same outcome—he was always one of the lucky survivors.

What Lev did not know was that this would be his final battle as a grunt. He had a one-way ticket out of hell—straight into Lucifer's cage.

The vehicle's engines blasted another wave of compressed air and it jetted away from Zone-10's airbase, not stopping until it reached the neutral zone to deliver its unholy freight.

Lev steeled his resolve and released himself onto the battlefield.

CHAPTER 6

HEARTS OF OBSIDIAN

"Who the fuck do you think you are, tiny?" said the leader, and the largest, of the three goons. His wart-covered face contorted into an ugly sneer.

Rak had to agree. *Why would such a small, cowardly creature like Gherm stand in the way of Vyrga's minions?* Rak wondered. As far as Rak knew, Gherm was not very friendly with any of the other weaklings, and even if he were, he would never stick his neck out for *anyone*, which was why Vyrga's minions targeted him at all. The only person Gherm would normally consider trying to save was Ghorza, but not even for her sake would he go head-to-head against any adversaries. In such a scenario, Gherm would simply beg them to leave her alone.

"I asked you, who the *fuck* do you think you are!" repeated the greyborn thug. He glared at the smaller greyborn who dared obstruct him. Gherm now wore a smug expression.

The leader stepped closer, intending to pressure Gherm to back down, but to no avail. The leader was confused that his strange adversary did not cower as expected. What was happening? It was easy to tell from Gherm's physique that he was no warrior. The leader briefly shot a glare at his past victims—they flinched on sight, for they, too, had no idea who this bogey was. The leader did not like being confused; his confusion only made him angrier.

Rak, still gawking, could make neither heads or tails of the confrontation. First, three of Vyrga's cronies had tried to pick a fight in Rak's territory. Second, Gherm, of all greyborns, now stood in their way.

And third, when the thugs had tried to threaten Gherm as well, he had simply regarded them as though he'd needed to take the garbage out. Rak bet that no one else in the crowd slowly gathering, including him, had any idea what was going on. This situation was just *bizarre*.

The fat goon, who had been standing behind his bewildered leader, finally broke the silence. "Hey, boss, I think I know who this is."

"Finally some fucking info! Lay it on me, mate!"

"This bugger's that bird Ghorza's brother! You know, the slag who refused to work for Vyrga," answered the goon with a grin. He did not notice the change in Gherm's expression, but his boss did.

"Oh!" chortled the head goon. "Look at this dipshit, you made him mad!" The warty bastard threw his head backwards in laughter, flashing his rotten teeth to the heavens, before he suddenly stopped laughing and glared at Gherm. "So what? We insulted that bitch sister of yours, what're ya gonna do about it? Nothin', 'cause now I know who you *really* are: that bludger who got hurt when the tunnel collapsed. Guess now you're a mute," he said, "and a retard, too."

Gherm was livid.

At this point, he'd usually flash a meek smile and try to apologize or something, thought Rak. *Did the damage from the collapse really affect his mind? Should I interfere?* Although Rak hated the company of weaklings, he had nothing against those who were physically or mentally disabled—he hadn't fallen that far yet. Like everyone else in the crowd, he was starting to pity the silent Gherm, but something in his mind told him that there was more going on than he was aware. His instincts were telling him that something was different about Gherm.

The head thug inched ever closer and lowered his head to stare eye-to-eye with this nuisance. "Do you wanna know what'll happen to her? After Vyrga clears this place of all the rabble standing in his way, she and everyone else who refused to bow down will suffer." A smile gradually creeped its way across its face. "Though, Vyrga's a reasonable man. If she refuses to give herself to him, he'll make her!"

"There is one thing I can do."

"Oh, so you *can* ta— *Ghrrrrr*!" gurgled the leader, grabbing his slit throat. He stumbled backwards a few steps and turned to his stunned compatriots for help before Gherm pulled the goon's face down to eye level.

"I can rid this world of unneeded filth," he snarled, exhaling emphatically onto the goon's face.

With an obsidian knife he had managed to conceal until now, Gherm repeatedly hacked away at his enemy's stomach. The head thug's entrails spilled onto the ground.

The dying thug gasped one last time, bloody tears falling down his face, as he departed from this world to the next.

Gherm turned to the two remaining thugs. "So. Wanna join your boss?"

"You killed him... You killed Varg!" blubbered the fat one, with his silent and easy-to-overlook companion able to do little more than nod in shock.

Can't blame him, thought Rak. *Who could've predicted that Gherm would butcher someone in cold blood?* It was not uncommon for a couple of greyborns to die in a fight, and the guards would turn a blind eye anyway. But a runt like Gherm had both emerged victorious against a group of Vyrga's men and taken out their leader in one attack, even if it was a cheap shot.

"Yes, I did. Let me ask again." Gherm made sure to enunciate clearly this time, taking a step forward with every word so the other two could not possibly mishear. "*Wanna join your boss?*"

"You have no idea what you just did, do you?" snarled the larger thug as he could stand neither the sight nor attitude of his friend's killer.

"I do. I not only interfered with Vyrga's business, but I also killed one of his men. Sure, he was expendable, but he was still Vyrga's, which means I'm now a target. But let's not forget that Vyrga wants my sister—so was I not already a target? *Are we not all targets?*" roared Gherm, stunning the crowd further.

He pointed his finger at the thugs and continued his speech. "*Every* time! *Every* single time, you attack us, harass us, and abuse us! And for what? Your stupid turf war? You keep targeting us even though we're not Rak's men just so you can pretend you're not the cowards you really are, making our already-miserable lives as slaves even more miserable! Even though you're also fellow slaves, fellow greyborns, you *prey* on us to inflate your own ego... but I say *enough* is *enough*!" he declared, spreading his arms wide in the air.

"Though I do not have the right to represent you, I *am* one of you. I suffer what you suffer, I feel the same pain you feel, I curse the same fate you curse, and I despair as you all despair. Don't we suffer enough for the sins of our ancestors? Do we *need* more suffering in our miserable, short lives? DO OUR LOVED ONES NEED MORE SUFFERING IN THEIR MISERABLE, SHORT LIVES?!"

Rak scratched his head. *Does he think anyone here would agree—*

"No!" yelled one slave, old and missing one eye, returning life to the stunned crowd.

Huh.

"We've had enough!"

Did he pay some people to sway the crowd?

"Get out of here, you bastards!"

Guess he did. Rak smiled amusedly.

"Pick on someone else, you pieces of shit!"

"Leave us alone!"

"Burn in hell, you animals!"

"Enough!" snapped the formerly-silent one, seething with rage as he pointed his knife at Gherm. "You think just because this wanker managed to kill Varg that you can take us on! Do you think that if you even think about taking us on, we'll let you go? We work for Vyrga! One of the sickest fucks in the entire world! You think that if you defy us, defy him, it'll end pretty? No, it won't! So once I gut this fucker like a pig, you better be ready to learn your place! You're all weaklings and your only value is to serve those who're stronger than you!"

The crowd began to waver as fear gripped their hearts. They had tried to act strong and stand up to their bullies, but it was an act. After all, they were as he described.

So now, they lower their heads? Typical, Rak lamented. *It's not like Vyrga would actually waste his time with common rabble. Nobody does. He'll most likely make an example out of the leaders.* His excitement in what could have been wilted into disgust at the mass display of cowardice. He knew these unaffiliated wimps would never stand up for themselves against a strong enemy, at least not without the backing of a stronger entity or a ready sacrifice. Rak guessed Gherm's diatribe was not enough to move them and he would never stick his neck out for their ilk again.

"*So what*?" retorted Gherm, drawing the crowd's attention once again. "So what if we're weak?"

Gherm turned toward Vyrga's men. "So what if you're stronger than us? Does that mean we should serve you? Does that mean we should grovel in the mud and let you step on us, feed off of us, rape our loved ones, and make our lives a nightmare for as long as we live? *No*! I *refuse* to live like that!" he exclaimed. "When I almost experienced death, my life flashed before my eyes—can you guess what I learned?"

He paused for barely a moment, the crowd entranced. "It's not worth living! An existence where I slave away for the likes of your 'master' isn't a life at all—it's hell! And since I'm already in hell, why shouldn't I fight? Why shouldn't we all fight? Yes, we're weak. Yes, we're cowardly. But together, we can accomplish the impossible! If we can't stand on our own two feet, we can lean on each other! In *our* numbers, there is *strength*!"

Gherm gave a final flourish. "So *lend* me your strength, and *I* shall lend you mine! *I* will be your sword and shield! And *I*," Gherm announced, hand over his heart, "shall lead us in the march to *reclaim our dignity*!"

"Gherm! Gherm! Gherm! Gherm!" roared the crowd in unison.

The two remaining thugs started to shudder in fear. As the fat one backed away, his wiry companion took a deep breath, steeled his nerves and charged forward, copper knife brandished in his left hand.

"Look out!" cried the old man from before, but Gherm, clutching his own knife in a hammer grip, had seen this coming.

The thug sliced downwards with his knife. Gherm dodged to the left out of harm's way and slashed in an upwards arc with his own knife, aiming for the inside of his opponent's wrist. The thug managed to move his arm just in time to evade before jumping backwards.

The crowd was mesmerized. Both adversaries circled around each other, waiting for opportunities to strike again.

The thug suddenly leapt again at Gherm, closing the distance in a moment, and lunged at Gherm's left wrist. Gherm deflected the attack with a swipe of his own, but not without sustaining a nasty gash on his left lower arm. Gherm clenched his jaw to maintain focus despite the pain.

Gherm lunged once more. By an unusual stroke of luck, his knife caught in his opponent's left shoulder. Gherm quickly twisted the embedded knife, shifted his weight onto his back foot, and kicked the thug down onto the ground an arm's length away from striking range. The fallen thug locked eyes with his rotund friend and silently called for help; his "friend" turned tail and fled.

Gherm immediately pounced onto his fallen opponent, wresting the thug's knife-clutching hand away and trying simultaneously to drive his own knife into his target's upper chest. The thug grabbed Gherm's right wrist.

The thug struggled against Gherm's pressure and almost managed to free his left hand, but the damage to his left shoulder had weakened his control on Gherm's right wrist. With a final grunt, Gherm plunged his obsidian blade into the thug's chest.

The thug howled and let go of his knife.

CHAPTER 7
RIDE TO GLORY

Finally. Step one was a success, Lev muttered to himself once he at last had a chance to sit down at home. *I hope Rak recognizes the value of our long-term partnership. Sometimes an agreement and a handshake is all you need to win, after all.*

Lev thought back to the fight.

* * *

Lev's breathing was ragged, his left arm was bleeding, and he was on top of the lifeless body of his foe. His knife was still lodged in the thug's heart.

Lev took a moment to compose himself. Then he pulled the knife out of the corpse and surveyed the immediate area, but failed to find the other thug.

This alarmed Lev. He could conceive of three possible reasons the other thug had not even tried to intervene: one, he had called for reinforcements; two, the enraptured crowd had taken him out themselves; or three, he had hidden himself somewhere else in the cave to watch the spectacle from a safe distance and ambush Lev once the crowd dispersed. Though Lev was on the verge of exhaustion, he acknowledged that from the little he had observed of those blindly loyal drones, he might not have any real reason to worry about retaliation.

Thankfully it was the second, as Lev soon found the wiry bogey beaten and bound near Rak and his men. As Lev stepped closer, the stone-faced Rak regarded him thoughtfully. It was clear to Lev what Rak sought from him.

"Looks like we need to talk," said Lev. Rak simply nodded.

Lev wiped his knife on the dead thug's pants before tearing himself a bandage from the dead thug's shirt.

Lev then stood up to face his audience, whose eyes were glued to him out of both fear and respect: fear of the possibility that Vyrga would retaliate, but also respect for the man who had taught them to challenge Vyrga's authority and resolved to protect them from their predators.

As though to answer their cry for guidance, Lev thrust his knife skywards with a rousing battle cry. "My brothers! We should *never* fear that mongrel Vyrga, for he and his men are few and we are many! Follow me, and I swear on my life he shall *never* threaten us again!"

At first, nobody spoke up. Vyrga likely would ignore them in normal circumstances, and perhaps even in circumstances as unusual as now, but if they followed Gherm too far, Vyrga would hunt and kill them and their families. They were certain that it would be safer to avoid getting involved at all.

Even so, a couple of greyborns wordlessly stepped forwards out of the crowd to face Lev. Slowly, an older greyborn stepped forwards as well, and turned to yell at the crowd. "What do you think you're doing! Is this a treatment a hero deserves?"

"He may be a hero to you," argued a youth from the crowd, "but that doesn't mean he's one to us. *We're* not the ones who are gonna get killed."

"Maybe not this time, but what about next time!" the elder argued back.

The youth was silent.

"Hah, I expected as much. Don't you get it? Even if Vyrga's goons had targeted someone else to deal with their boredom, they could target us any day. Who knows. In the future, maybe I'll get attacked, maybe you. Maybe your brother, your father, your uncle, or anyone you care about. As long as we are weak and divided, anyone could pick on us!" Lev watched the elder feign tears. "If all it takes for my grandchildren to be able to rise above the lot of a greyborn is to follow this 'Gherm' fellow... then by the gods, I will do it!"

A wave of murmurs washed over the masses in front of Lev before briefly giving way to a still silence.

"He's right, isn't he?" volunteered one man.

"He is. And if we don't do anything, nothing will change, right?" affirmed another.

"Then let's go for it!"

"I think I'll pass. The risks aren't worth it—"

"What are you saying? They definitely are!"

"Hey, I'll fight with him! Beats being a target."

"Hope, you have a spot open for me—I've been meaning to teach those bastards a lesson!"

"Sadly, I'm too old to fight, but I'll do my best to help, Gherm."

"Thanks for saving my brother, Gherm!"

Over time the talks and speeches turned into triumphant chants, filling the cave with the sound of the name Lev had been made to take as a goblin. *Gherm sure is lucky I'm pulling the strings*, thought Lev as he basked in the chorus of cheers. Everything, save for the initial hesitation of the crowd, was going according to his plan so far. He was thankful he had made sure to get that favour from the right elder beforehand.

When Lev was satisfied, he raised his hands to silence them and made his tone humble. "No need to thank me. More importantly, we have some work to do, now, isn't that right?"

Most of the crowd abruptly turned to check the nearby post normally occupied by their supervisors.

The post was empty.

The herd of greyborns began to whisper and curse anxiously before splitting off to search for their mining supervisor Thorst. However, they soon found him standing in the front row of the crowd, looking miffed. "Had your fun, eh? Now get back to work!" he roared. Every slave but Gherm hurriedly returned to their tasks.

"Hey, Thorst," greeted Gherm amiably.

"Hey, Gherm," Thorst reciprocated, "how's Ghorza?" He furrowed his brow. "And how are you planning to explain to her what just happened?"

"That will be hard, but I think I can manage."

Thorst shook his head. "Whatever. I hope you *manage* not to get skinned alive. It's *Vyrga*, after all." Thorst went back to his post.

Lev sighed. It was fortunate for everyone in the mines that Thorst had been the one on duty during the debacle with Vyrga's goons. Thorst was one of the more easy-going supervisors, and as a protégé of Kul's, he and Gherm were quite friendly.

"So is it my turn?" asked a voice behind Lev.

"Yes, Rak. It is," answered an exasperated Gherm.

The larger-than-average bogey stared down at his scrawny, greyborn counterpart with his arms crossed. The smaller bogey looked up at him.

"It must be my lucky day. I've been graced with an audience with the mighty Gherm," teased Rak.

"And blessed *me*. My humble self was granted the honour of meeting with the amazing Rak," bickered Lev.

They scowled at each other for a moment before bursting into laughter at the same time.

"Hahaha! You're good!" Rak told Lev. It had been a long time since anyone had had the gall to talk back to Rak like that.

"I know. So are you." Lev rapidly regained his composure. "But really now, let's start our discussion, all right?"

Rak nodded. He, Lev, and Hem were about to discuss a possible alliance, but Rak remembered he needed to get rid of the last of Vyrga's lackeys. He walked to the bruised hostage and snapped his fingers. One of his minions grabbed the hostage by the ears and raised his head, exposing his neck.

The ashen-faced hostage struggled against his restraints. "P-Please... By the grace of Vyrga, please let me go..."

Sadly, Rak knew that showing mercy to one of Vyrga's hangers-on, especially one as brainwashed as this, was pointless. The bastard would probably run back to Vyrga in shame before returning, further brainwashed, to terrorize the slaves again. Rak raised his own knife, a copper knife he had pilfered from a corpse a week ago, and prepared to end his captive's life.

"Wait!" Lev frantically threw his arms out between Rak and the captive.

"What the hell do you think you're doing?" countered Rak. He had every intention to deal the finishing blow himself, and he was greatly insulted that Gherm now seemed ready to order him to step back.

"I believe we should let him go."

Lev's proposal shocked everyone within earshot. *Let one of Vyrga's men go? Was that a joke?* Even the thug himself was astonished. Vyrga never showed mercy to his subordinates. He had even killed those who'd shown anyone mercy in creative ways to indoctrinate his followers properly.

Rak spoke up. "I thought maybe getting hit in the head made you brave, not foolish. You want to show him mercy? It's Vyrga we're talking about."

"I'm not showing mercy. I'm sending a warning."

"A warning to Vyrga?" muttered Hem, astounded. No *slave or commoner has ever survived that. A noble, sure, but not an upstart greyborn with no protection.*

"Yeah, a warning. Vyrga's bound to find me no matter what, since everyone here knows me now. As for him," Lev gestured vaguely at the sniveling hostage, "whether we kill him or not, Vyrga will already be insulted enough to hunt me down. Why not provoke him into a trap?" Lev hoped the prisoner would interpret his statements not as a bluff, but rather as a credible threat that the bogey "Gherm" could take Vyrga down.

In any case, Gherm, Rak, and Hemgall all knew that Vyrga was too cautious to charge blindly into an enemy. He preferred to study them, then strike with prudence. "After all," Gherm continued, "showing mercy to a victim of this cursed life cannot possibly be a sin. We all eventually fall to our lowest point, and we all feel helpless to change anything sometimes. We all find ourselves desperate to get stronger by any means, and, well, some of us resort to crime."

Rak perceived that this was a jab at him, but he chose to ignore it.

"But I believe any goblin should be given at least one chance to redeem himself. For even if we sink into darkness, we can still swim our way back to the surface."

Lev gauged his impromptu audience's reactions—with the exception of the thug, no one was that impressed—and quickly added, "Besides, to Vyrga, it'll be a slap in the face. And it isn't a secret that he's needed one for a long time." A few chuckles and nods, and Lev knew he had succeeded.

"You're playing a dangerous game, boy. I like it," commended Hem.

"Thanks, um…"

"Hemgall. But you can call me Hem. That's what people with balls call me. And you got a big pair of bronze ones, kid."

"Thanks, Hem." Lev turned to Rak. "Can you do me a favour and let him go?"

"It's your funeral," Rak conceded before ordering his men to untie the grateful thug and throw him out of Rak's territory.

"Glad that's over. Let's talk."

* * *

Sadly, my work isn't done yet, Lev mumbled as his consciousness returned to the present. He stood up from the chair.

He had negotiated a deal with Rak: Rak would once again provide protection to the weaklings in his territory and help Lev secure the capital and assets necessary to establish his own faction. In return, their factions would be allies; Lev would, according to tradition, serve as a vassal to Rak and aid him in eliminating his rivals, provided rendering aid would not result in the annihilation of Lev's faction. Lev's group would also guard the border between Rak's and Vyrga's territories and could lay claim to only a third of the rewards during joint operations.

Most importantly, Lev would pay tribute to Rak every two weeks, or fourteen days.

He filled a large bowl with water, then proceeded to wash himself and his clothes of all the accumulated blood, dust, and grime. He also replaced his bandages before patting himself dry and changing into a cleaner set of rags.

At last, he lay down in his bed and placed the knife on the floor within arm's reach.

As Lev closed his eyes, ready to drift off to sleep, the door slammed open, startling him awake. He swiftly seized the knife and jumped out of the bed, rolling fluidly into a combat stance with his knife pointed at the intruder.

Lev was so on edge that it took him a full breath cycle to recognize Ghorza in the doorway, panicking and in tears.

"What have you done!" she screamed.

"Done what?"

"Don't play dumb! Everyone's talking about it! Why did you doom us by killing Vyrga's men?!"

"I had no choice."

Silence blanketed the room.

"What kind of excuse is *that*? Your 'grand' speech won over so many bogeys—you basically have an army to die with you now!"

Lev inhaled as though to speak up, but Ghorza cut him off. "But that's just what you had *planned*, right? I'm not stupid, Gherm—no, whoever you are…" Her voice trailed off.

Lev knew Ghorza was right, but his heart still ached. Those were not words Gherm had ever wanted to hear.

"You wanted this," Ghorza continued, her voice cracking. "You wanted to raise an army of the unfortunate for your own use." Her eyes burned holes into Lev's soul in their desperate search for any trace of her brother. "And judging by the look on your face… You may not be Gherm, but he's in there somewhere, right?"

Lev's sole desire in his new life was to leave his mark upon this world; Gherm, who refused to detach himself, was simply… *interfering* with his emotional regulation. In contrast to Lev, Gherm's only wish was for his sister and him to live happily. Though Gherm's wish was less ambitious, his love for his sister was strong enough to embed itself into Lev's soul, and despite only having known her for two days, Lev felt that Ghorza was infinitely important to him.

Lev exhaled deeply with resignation. "You're right, and wrong, at the same time." Before she could verbalize another question, he raised a hand and spoke again. "The reason I'm doing all this is to protect the one goblin I care about—you."

"Me? But you're not the same Gherm I know."

"Not fully, yes. But it's just as you said before. I might be different, but in a way, I'm still your brother, so please don't reject me," he implored, something the unadulterated Lev would never have done under any circumstances.

Ghorza paused to collect her thoughts. She understood that "Gherm" was not her younger brother anymore. She knew he was someone different. But unlike the impostor she had encountered yesterday, the bogey now before her pleading not to reject him was identical to the Gherm she remembered.

She even felt that the original Gherm himself wanted her to accept this. Without her, he might one day disappear.

After a moment of quiet contemplation, she relaxed her guard and extended her hand to him "Fine... bro."

"Thanks, sis." He grabbed her hand and pulled her into a hug.

"Still early for this, but I'll make an exception." She returned the hug with some reluctance. "And I'm still going to keep calling you Gherm, but can you tell me your other name?" she requested, evidently still afraid that her brother was possessed.

A demon of Mal, the goddess of deception, was capable of tricking both the heart and mind. However, it was also fated to do either of two things when queried for its true name: speak its name, binding itself as a servant to those who heard it, or bluntly refuse to reveal its name and undo the possession it had painstakingly carried out.

Lev chuckled at Ghorza's superstitiousness, but entertained it anyway. "His name was Leonard Erand Vandersteen, but people called him Lev."

"Then hit yourself, Lev," she ordered cheekily.

"Nope."

"Good enough for me," she giggled before both of them burst into laughter.

"Oh, and before you ask, the reason I killed those two instead of doing something more discreet was that they had told me Vyrga is planning to make you his concubine."

"*What!*"

* * *

Pog, one of Vyrga's thugs, was still shocked as he made his way home. That peewee, Gherm, had seen into his soul.

Vyrga had expanded his territorial influence a year ago and imposed taxes on all households whose heads did not work for him. While Pog had resisted at first, the protection fees had slowly grown too heavy a financial burden. Five months ago he had joined Vyrga's gang to put food on the table for his wife and three children, and he had regretted it ever since.

As time passed, though, he had learned to desensitize himself to the constant guilt polluting his mind, and had come to prefer cheap thrills to the company of his family. Nowadays, he spent most of his time drunk between the legs of desperate whores whose households were unable to pay Vyrga's taxes. Transferring merits to his family was now little more than a chore he occasionally remembered to do. But after hearing Gherm's speech...

"What the fuck am I doing with my life? What the fuck am I doing to my family? What the fuck have I done to other families?" He had convinced himself that he no longer felt guilty for his actions, but the truth was that he had locked the guilt away in a corner of his mind; now the gates were breaking open.

"Oh, gods... What kind of fuckwit have I been? I had thought that I didn't give a rat's arse about my actions, but here I am feeling like dog shit..."

Halfway home, Pog stood still with his head in his hands, remembering all the horrible things he had done, all the pain he had caused his friends and family, and all the suffering he had inflicted upon others.

"No... It's not too late! I can fix this!" he yelled, determination in his voice, causing bystanders to look at him in confusion before continuing on his way.

Shit... Yelling out loud? I really am dumb as a box of rocks, he thought while flushed with embarrassment. *No time to kick myself in the balls though. I gotta go get my family. In the next few days, that shitcunt Vyrga will launch a raid on the eastern gangs; we gotta pack our stuff and sneak outta this shithole by then. Helga, I'm gonna fix everything.*

Pog straightened his back and marched home with the fires of hope in his eyes.

* * *

"Good morning, Ghorza," greeted Lev with a smile.

For as long as Ghorza could remember, she had always woken up before Gherm had. Then she remembered his confession the day before. *This'll take some getting used to*, she thought to herself.

She stiffly returned his greeting. "Morning, bro."

Lev tried not to laugh. Even though he had survived meron powder two days ago and given her his "true" name yesterday, she had still tried to check whether he was a demon. On a surface level, she believed him; below the surface, she still feared that he was one. When she had made Lev chant a few religious hymns, he had complied, but when she had subsequently demanded that he submerge his hands, or rather dip his fingers, in the meagre reserve of salt they kept in the house, Lev had run out of patience—and seen an opportunity to mess with her.

The moment his claws had pierced the surface of the salt reserve, he had screamed as if in pain, nearly giving Ghorza a heart attack, before cackling uncontrollably at her frightened expression. In return, Ghorza had punched the wind out of him.

They prepared breakfast, then sat down to eat. Compared to the sectioned cave worm Lev would rather have forgotten, this meal was more austere, consisting of watered-down porridge made from unidentified grains, a few common insects, mushrooms, and turnips.

While the two siblings could normally spare only a few merits here and there to feed themselves, Ghorza permitted them to indulge every now and then with food sourced from either deeper levels of the cavern or imported from outside the cavern entirely. Of food from deeper within the cavern, insects and mushrooms were cheap and readily obtainable; the fuzzy cave worm from two days prior was a major indulgence, significantly more expensive than insects and mushrooms. Of food from outside the cave, grains cost less than vegetables, including turnips which, for vegetables, were still quite cheap.

"So are you sure you wanna go to the mining quarters?" asked Ghorza between bites. She pointed at Lev's bandage. "How are you going to work with that wound? Doesn't it hurt?"

"Of course it hurts, but I have to go. We need all the merits we can get, and if I want to build up my reputation, I have to show up. Also, I need to discuss something important with Rak."

"Fine. But make sure not to get into any more trouble. I wish I could stay home with you until you recovered. It would be safer for you that way."

"Safety... Ah! Though it's expensive, make sure to bring home some blocks of wood, a good knife for carving wood, some copper nails, and a hammer today."

Ghorza was dumbfounded. "Why in the world would we need that crap? You're neither a carpenter nor an artist, so why do you suddenly want to bankrupt us?"

"For safety concerns. I could strengthen the door at the entrance of the house to prevent undesirables from breaking in."

"It's already a wooden door, Gherm. Everyone else uses rags or leather to cover their doorways and they don't get robbed, so why would we? Do you know why nobody here gets robbed? 'Cause we're all poor! Who on earth would steal from slaves? And what would they steal, insects and veggies!"

Lev narrowed his eyes at the stubborn girl. "It's not about stealing, it's about murder and arson. This house is made from wood, and we're made of flesh, muscles, and bones. In case you hadn't noticed, wood can be burned and we can be killed, especially in our sleep."

"And I'm saying nobody will come inside and kill us. Vyrga's a wretch, but he's not stupid. Our dad, may he rest in the cycle, chose this very spot because it was the safest. You might not remember, but he was as paranoid as you currently are. He worked hard for enough merits to build the house near to the guard station and he made sure to buy the sturdiest wood available for the door."

"I'm just saying—"

"We already block it on the inside with a large rock at night. What more do you want? Besides, if you're that afraid of someone getting in, what about the windows? They're large enough to let out the smoke from our cooking, so they're definitely large enough for anyone to crawl through them."

"With the exception of Kul and his apprentices, the guards here aren't very reliable and could be bribed. As for the windows, I've already thought of them and we can make some sort of alarm system for them. We'll block them too once we're done with it. The highest priority right now is the door."

"Seriously?" Ghorza rolled her eyes. "Listen, I'm not gonna blow our life savings on your paranoia! Even if we block the door, any group of maniacs with axes can just chop through it. Heck, even a large hammer would work. It would take longer, but it would still work."

"Alright, alright. I get it. But I'm still going to bolster our security once I get enough merits. Even a bar handle for the door would be better than nothing."

"I don't know what a... bar handle is, but sure. As long as we don't starve, you can knock yourself out."

They quietly finished their meal and went out to receive their assignments. It was the same as last time, except Kul was more worried about Lev due to his injury. Normally slaves were forced to keep working until the taskmaster decided it was enough, but Kul gave Lev permission to leave early if his injury proved prohibitive.

As Lev walked into the mining quarter, he was showered with praise from fellow slaves who had watched the fight the previous day. They regarded him with respect and adoration as they observed his small, damaged, yet regal form. He held his head high and proud, yet unlike the warriors and nobles, he never ignored anyone who tried to talk to him no matter how wretched they looked. No matter what people thought of him before, he was now a leader, and he was shown respect befitting one.

"Hey, Gherm!" hollered a voice from afar.

Who is this bogey who dares talk to him so casually? thought many slaves concurrently, only to panic at the bogey revealing himself.

"Hey, Hem," replied Gherm with a friendly smile.

Hem! It was Hemgall! many slaves screamed in their minds before they realized it made perfect sense. Yesterday, after the fight and Lev's talk with Rak, Rak's men had not only collected fewer merits than usual, but had also resumed protecting and helping the other bogeys as they had done in the past.

"Hey, you slackers, get back to work!" yelled a taskmaster. The bogeys returned their attention to their respective tasks.

As Hem approached Lev, he leaned in and whispered, "There's

something important that Rak needs to tell you."

Lev's smile faded and was replaced with a determined look. He nodded at Hem and they snuck away to meet with Rak at the northwestern side of the first floor of the mining quarters.

"Right on time," said Rak. "So Gherm, how's your arm?"

Lev smiled ruefully. "Fine and dandy. Could still use a week or two. How's life?"

"Shitty as always. And you better hope that arm heals fast, considering what'll happen in two weeks."

Lev's blood ran cold. "What's going to happen in two weeks?"

Rak smiled wryly. "Another expedition."

CHAPTER 8

WEAPONS AND SLAVES

"Thrust!" commanded Lev.

More than twenty bogeys thrust blunt wooden spears forwards almost, but not quite, in unison.

Two weeks had passed since Rak's announcement, and today would have been the day they set out on another expedition. Fortunately, the Jiira had had to repel an attack by the Kur just a week ago, and the leader of this expedition had been heavily injured in the defence. Rak had only received word four days ago that the expedition was delayed for an additional three weeks from today.

Thank goodness for small miracles, thought Lev. It had taken him a week and a half to teach his bogeys to follow basic commands and stand in formation, and even then, they could not maintain formation longer than a second.

Accordingly, Lev had changed his lesson plan: his men were to fight in three-man groups, each consisting of two spear wielders and a shield bearer. The shield bearer would draw the enemy's attention and block their attacks. At the same time, one of the spear wielders would thrust at the enemy's feet while the other thrust at a vital point such as the chest or head. It was hardly a sophisticated formation and would probably make military experts cringe, but it was simple enough for these complete rookies to master it in time for the expedition. Lev would have improved it if he had more time, men, and resources, but sadly, his group had just gained its thirty-second member three days ago.

Lev's left arm itched underneath the bandage, but he resisted the urge to scratch. The gash was healing as well as it could; he estimated it would need just another week to heal into a nasty scar.

If only I had more time, I could train some archers, too, he quietly lamented. Most greyborn hunters relied on traps, javelins, and melee weapons rather than bows and arrows to hunt; archery required flexible wood and feathers for fletching, both of which were difficult to procure in a cave. Understandably, archers were quite rare underground, and the few who did make appearances were almost always accompanying nobles, or at least were goblins themselves.

"Gher— I mean, sir!" Volker, one of the younger trainees, called out to Lev. Volker had been one of the first to join Lev's faction and had visibly trained the hardest. It was he and his brother whom Vyrga's lackeys had targeted when Lev had interfered. Volker saw Lev as a hero; Volker's brother had thought otherwise.

"What?" Lev asked the youth in an agitated tone. Nothing was going the way he had planned, and he had a hunch that nothing Volker was about to tell him would help.

"U-Uhm..." The youth stuttered and trailed off.

"Get on with it, Volker. It's not like it can get worse than—"

"Ow!" interrupted one of the new recruits, who was trying to eavesdrop. "What was *that* for?" One of his comrades was turning around and had accidentally hit him.

"Sorry!"

And that's why they're training with blunt spears, Lev remembered, shaking his head.

"Um... Mr. Gherm— I-I mean... Sir?"

"*Yes*, Volker?"

"I've never fought before, but I've seen some guards cull hivelings. Wouldn't it be better to get some ranged support?"

"Of *course* it would be better to get some ranged support. Concentrated volleys are deadly. But we can't get archers. The stingy upper class and the goblins have a monopoly on them," Lev complained.

"P-P-Please remember not to insult them to their faces, sir." Volker reminded Lev for the twentieth time since he joined Lev's group. "And what's a... mo-no-po-ly?"

"I'd never do something that stupid, and to answer your question, in simple terms a monopoly is when a single person or a group of people have full control over a resource, so they alone can decide who can and cannot access it. Sadly, according to Rak, that piece of shit Vyrga's got four archers, while Rak and we haven't got squat, hence the wooden helmets and chest guards." Lev had used all the merits he had earned over the past week and a half to furnish whatever he could for his troops, and had managed to convince Rak to donate old equipment to fill in the gaps.

"Why not use slings or javelins?"

"Rocks shot from slings are too weak to harm a hiveling's body, and how many javelins can the average grey bogey carry? Eight to ten?"

"That's something I keep wondering about, why *rocks*? If we tweak them, can't slings be attached to a wooden body and used as bows to shoot arrows?"

Lev's eyes lit up. "Slingshots? Oh! Nice idea," Lev commended. But his joy faded as quickly as it had arrived.

"W-What's wrong, sir?" asked the lad nervously.

"We can't make arrows because we lack fletching," Lev grunted through clenched teeth. "Not to mention that we can't make slingshots because we don't have rubber. Lucky us!" he declared, throwing his hands up in exasperation.

"Rubber?"

Damn! I shouldn't have said that, Lev thought. *How could these primitives, let alone I, a greyborn slave, know what rubber is?* He now had to come up with an answer that would satisfy the curious lad without also giving him any reason to suspect Gherm was anything other than a greyborn slave.

Lev made a show of furtively scanning their surroundings. "I heard a rumour that an exiled shaman has created a wondrous and flexible material that he calls 'rubber.' It's extremely stretchy, yet durable," he whispered into the young bogey's ear. "From what I know, after the discovery, the nobles hunted him down, and once they caught him, they hid his invention from the public eye and killed him. We shouldn't take this any further, agreed?"

Volker nodded vigorously—nobody wanted to end up on the nobles' bad side.

"Good." Lev was relieved that the lad believed his lie, as he certainly wouldn't have believed it himself.

"So slings it is, sir?"

"Yup. There's nothing wrong with them as a ranged weapon. They're user-friendly, deadly within the range we'd use them, and versatile enough to launch almost anything, but hivelings and heavily armoured creatures would just shake off the rocks we'd sling at them. If we had something better than rocks for ammo, that would be great, perhaps some form of metal projectiles, but the goblins and the nobles prevent us from using metal, so we only have rocks," Lev rambled. "Unless we want to be creative, in which case we could try clay bottles—"

"Clay bottles?" This was the first time Volker had heard of people using clay bottles as weaponry.

"That's right. You can fill them with all kinds of nasty surprises. Paralyzing poison, sleeping powder, you name it. You can even fill them with oil and set your enemies on fire." Lev smiled at the idea of setting his enemies on fire, but that smile did not persist.

"Sadly, useful quantities of poison, powder, and oil cost more than we can afford, and don't even think we can afford even a drop of cyfrac oil." Cyfracs were a rare family of plants, found on the fifth floor and below, that resembled a red-colored rye and were easily combustible. Their oil had many uses from ceremonies to smithing, but was most valued by shamans and healers because its flames spread fast and lasted a long time.

"But it's so useful!"

"Yes, it is useful, but we can't get it. Even if we could, our supply would be limited. The best thing for a rope sling would be metal rounds, but we can't get those either."

Lev and Volker silently watched the new recruits train.

"Maybe we can," Volker piped up suddenly.

"How?"

"Would lead rounds work?"

"Absolutely. A good lead shot could pierce a bronze helmet. But I checked with Rak and other sources. Though we greyborns are allowed to use lead, we can only obtain it in ore form, and there are no weapon masters or smiths who deal with greyborns, unless you count the lowliest of craftsmen. And even *they* can't forge for themselves—they have to request smiths to cast the pieces, which they just assemble, decorate, and sell." Lev had searched high and low for ways greyborns could arm themselves better, but had discovered no leads.

"I know someone."

"*What?*" Lev nearly shouted, shocking his nearby troops.

He turned, calming them down, before returning his attention to Volker.

"He's an exile that my dad saved a long time ago. I can get him to help us, but knowing his personality, he won't do it for free. The only thing I can assure you of is that it won't be too pricey."

"*That* I can work with," remarked Lev excitedly.

"B-But there's one problem," stuttered Volker. He knew how much Lev hated the word "but."

"Which is?"

"That he refuses to reveal his identity to anyone but my dad and a select few, so only I can see him." Volker was surprised at how quickly he had explained the situation, and he worried that Gherm considered his abruptness rude. "S-Sorry, sir."

"Let me guess, he used to be some great and arrogant smith, but he pissed off some nobles who wanted him dead, not just exiled, so he hid in the only place someone of his calibre would ever avoid—the slave quarters. Right?" Lev intentionally matched Volker's conversational pace from earlier. "And his reason for hiding isn't just that those nobles are after him, but also that his already-damaged ego cannot handle anyone else recognizing his former identity."

"H-How did you know, sir?"

"I have a... *gift* when it comes to these sorts of things." *And it's a common scenario in games and novels,* Lev thought to himself shamelessly. He had never enjoyed wasting his time on frivolous activities such as gaming and reading fantasy, but Brutus had. He would always tell Lev about the plotlines of his favorite games, novels, and comics, even though Lev had never displayed the slightest interest. He now wished he had—knowing a few of those reincarnation scenarios would actually have helped him right about now. "Anyway, after training, go and cut us a deal. Lead projectiles would be a game-changer!"

"Really?" replied Volker, bewildered.

"Yeah, really. Now go!"

"Yes, sir!" Volker saluted before running back to his snickering companions.

Lev glared at Volker's associates. "You find this funny?" he snarled.

"N-N-N-No!" the now-pale trainees replied.

"'No,' *what?*"

"No, sir!"

"Good! Then straighten your backs, get into positions and run five laps around the mining quarters!"

"Yes, sir!" the men shouted with all their hearts.

More than a week under Lev had taught them how to respond to his orders and what kind of punishment they could expect if they defied him.

"And don't forget your spears!"

"Yes, sir!" his poor soldiers shakily answered back, about to break into tears.

Lev grinned. Playing the role of a sergeant from hell was quite fun.

As the recruits began their run, Lev joined them. He needed to be fit for battle as well, after all.

* * *

Lev had given Volker permission to leave immediately after he finished his laps, and soon after, Volker contacted him. as he was waiting for Lev outside his house.

Volker showed Lev a few samples from the smith, lead bullets the size of his thumb that had been masterfully crafted in various shapes. They mainly came in either the form of flat, elongated bullets with sharpened ends or oblong ones with one pointy and one round end each. They were all adorned with the symbol of the war god Jorm and artistic carvings in a way that wouldn't hamper their performance.

As much as Lev liked their designs, looks alone would not secure any victories. Lev stepped back into his house, retrieved a spare wooden helmet from his room, and returned outside where Volker was waiting, and gently placed the helmet on the ground a short distance away from any of the homes.

Lev pulled out a sling he had prepared for the occasion. He tied a slip knot, slid his middle finger into the loop, and pinched the handle between his forefinger and thumb. Closing his eyes, he cleared his mind of any distractions. Then he opened his eyes, placed an oblong bullet into the pouch, and drew the missile back into a wide vertical orbit.

He raised his arm and swung it down behind his head, tightening the first orbit before taking a pitcher's step. As the missile reached the top of its second orbit, he completed a step forward and released the handle as his wrist snapped forward, releasing the bullet.

Volker gasped as the speeding bullet raced forward, looking to pierce through the helmet with all its might.

Bang!

The bullet missed the helmet by a margin, cracking a large stone an arm's length behind it on impact instead.

They darted closer to examine the bullet. It was slightly deformed from the front, but had held together.

"Volker."

"Yes, Mr. Gherm— I mean sir!"

"Tell him that we'll need a lot of bullets, but drop the decorations," Lev told him with a smile.

"Y-Yes, sir!" replied the youth with vigour before marching towards the smith.

* * *

"So how was your day?" Ghorza asked Lev during a wonderful dinner of insects, porridge, and turnips.

"It was good. I managed to cross a few things off my agenda," he replied. It really had been a good day.

"Great, well my day was pretty hectic. To earn some extra merits, I worked harder than I already do, to a degree that even our overseer was surprised. She kept telling me to take a break. You know you're working hard when the person who's supposed to make you work harder tells you to take a break, right?"

"Yeah, That's right."

"I know. So I began telling her why I'm doing this and how you..."

While Ghorza prattled on and on, Lev thought back on how he had managed to secure both much-needed resources and ranged weaponry.

It's a good thing those greyborns know how to use slings, he thought. Most bogeys supplemented their diet by knocking down critters off the cavern ceiling. *Now I just need to teach them how to use slings in combat.*

"Wouldn't you agree?" Ghorza asked.

"Yeah, sure," he replied. *I do need to expand the number of formations though. Basic formations like a phalanx always have a fatal weakness which in its case is that its flanks are exposed to attacks and it's quite rigid, making applying any changes, or even turning, hard. Historically, that weakness was solved when a great conqueror thought of applying light infantry battalions which among their main functions was protecting the flanks. But we're lacking in numbers...*

"Are you even paying attention?" Ghorza said with a glare.

"Yeah, sure," he replied. *Maybe I could—*

"Gherm!"

"Wha— huh?"

"You've been spacing out a lot," Ghorza said, worried.

"Sorry, I've just had a lot on my plate. You know, due to our current circumstances."

"I know. Just... stay out of trouble, okay?"

"Don't worry about me. You should worry about yourself more. You look like you're gonna fall asleep right now."

"You're not the only one working hard, and one of us needs to save some extra merits," she nagged while shooting him a look, "because *some* ambitious bloke keeps spending all of his."

"Sorry, not sorry. It's for a better future."

"I hope. Are you done eating? We should sleep soon."

"Sure. But wash your hands first."

"I got it already! Sheesh." She had become more accustomed to Lev's antics recently.

They tidied the dining table, washed up, and went to bed early.

Lev, too, had become more accustomed to sleeping on Gherm's rickety bed, and promptly fell into a deep slumber.

Regrettably, however, he was unable to sleep as long as he had wanted—early the next morning, he was awoken by a scream from the dining area. He immediately grabbed his knife and rushed in, finding a teary-eyed Ghorza kneeling speechless, staring at the dining table. Her hands covered her mouth as she resisted the urge to puke.

On the table were three heads: one from the fat thug and two small enough to have come from young bogeys. Their untarnished faces were frozen in pain and anguish.

Looks like I need to secure the house after all, thought Lev.

CHAPTER 9

A RAT'S WILL

Inside a small room filled with wooden carvings and a few carving knives, a forlorn, middle-aged greyborn played a sad tune that spoke of the misery of life.

Greyborns outside his circle would wonder how he had learned to play the flute; the upper class of bogeys would wonder why he had chosen to learn the flute. Not that there was anything wrong with flutes in general, but in bogey society, flutes belonged in the hands of priests and poets, while warriors and nobles preferred the lur. But this bogey was neither priest nor poet, neither warrior nor noble. He was a greyborn, but not just any greyborn. He was a leader.

He played his tune while pondering the joke that was life, especially his own. His miserable life during which he had been rejected by his highborn father because of his grey skin. His miserable life during which his greyborn mother had blamed him for ruining hers. His miserable life during which he had suffered beating after beating from the brute she had married not only to hide the truth of his birth, but also to increase her own standing within the greyborn caste. His miserable life during which he had endured daily insults and beatings from their neighbours, who had hated that "father" but feared retaliation from the gang he led.

Fortunately, there was one way to release their aggressions his father sanctioned: taking their anger out on the boy through verbal and physical beatings.

He had grown up accepting misery as normal. He had rarely cried, but when he did, neither god nor man had answered. As such, he had understood from a young age that he was alone and his pain did not matter. Nothing mattered.

He had never expected his life to change, but one day, something had catalyzed a dramatic shift in his perspective.

In his early teens, to pay back some of the debt he "owed" his family for raising him, he had been forced to fight in a gambling ring prepared by the brute's gang.

Night after night, he would walk home, battered after winning a fight against a small, captured hiveling. Along the way, he would see a few of the neighbourhood boys amusing themselves with rat fights. By depriving the rats of food, the boys turned them aggressive, and for a while, the rats fought each other for the boys' scraps.

One night, one of the rats had finally snapped and bit its owner's fingers.

Seeing this, the teen had come to a realization. *If even an animal can't accept a life like this... then how can I?* He had then seen the boys kill the rebellious rat.

The teen feared death—he conjectured the rat had as well—but dreams of liberation had blossomed inside his heart regardless. Every day he had observed the rats revolt, and his heart revolted with them. Every day the neighbourhood ringmasters, too prideful to be bested by rodents, had killed more rats, yet more had bitten back.

Why do they fight knowing that they can't win? Why choose defiance over life? he had quietly inquired of them. As he'd watched the last rat, pocket knife stuck in its side, snarl in defiance down to its last twitch, it had clicked in his mind.

I don't have to live like this. I can free myself. Even if I suffer for my insolence, so what? I'm already suffering. Even if I get killed, so what? I'll eventually die someday. Even if I'll be cursed by the gods for parricide, so what? By what right can the gods, who ignore not only me but so many

*more, decide that I must live through this hell? They can shove their laws
up their asses!*

In that moment, he had sworn to not abide by anyone else's laws,
orders, or moral codes ever again for as long as he lived.

Then, he had steeled his resolve and plotted his parents' demise.

At the time, he might have been naïve in the ways of the world, but
he had been no fool. He had predicted that although he could win in a
one-on-one fight against his bastard of a stepfather, he would sustain
severe injuries and be left at the mercy of his mother.

So, he had concocted a simpler plan. Had his parents cared enough
to notice his inclination, the plan would have fallen through, but they
had been too complacent in their delusion that they would always
control him.

He had begun by poisoning their food. He hadn't used a lethal
poison, but rather a sleeping agent that he had stolen from an herbalist
peddling their wares near the ring. His stepfather's henchmen had
ridiculed him as his father's little slave boy his whole life, but they had
also respected his strength. He now sought to seize their loyalty.

In the dead of night, blood-curdling screams had woken many from
their sleep. They had rushed out from their homes to see what the
commotion was, only to wish that they had never seen it—the old
crime boss screeching from pain as his own "son" hacked off his arms
and legs at their joints with a stone-headed axe. And that wasn't all—
his son had then skinned the boss alive. True, the neighbours had hated
the old bastard, wanted him dead, and were painfully aware of what he
had done to the boy on a daily basis, but this was too much, too *cruel.*

That night, many of them had vomited onto the ground as though
seeking to purge their minds; those who had willed themselves not to
vomit after watching the child slaughter his "father" invariably lost the
second battle of wills when he did the same to his mother.

The boy had surveyed the crowd, focusing intently at the gathering of thugs frozen in horror at what had become of their leader, and spoken. "Tonight you witnessed the end of the old pig. Now tell me... Whom do you now serve?"

With that, a new leader had been born, and his name was—

"Oy, boss!" yelled a male voice as the door slammed open, disrupting the flow of both the music and the flutist's recollection.

"Os! You'd better have something important, or it's *your* head that's going to be rolling today," threatened Vyrga. He hated it when people interrupted his performances.

Oswald, nicknamed Os, chuckled. He was sure that most goblinoids would be shocked to learn that one of the bloodiest gang leaders among the greyborns spent his free time not only playing the flute, but also carving wood and writing poetry. If they heard he was carving something, they would assume he was carving the living skull of a virgin maiden into a new cup, not carving a chunk of wood into the shape of a bird, whatever a bird was.

Well, that's the type of guy he makes himself out to be, Os sighed. He, on the other hand, knew another side of Vyrga, the side that had practically raised him.

During the early days of his gang leadership, Vyrga had sought to build his own group of loyal subordinates to replace the majority of the old bastard's circle. So he had searched for other abandoned noble bastards like himself and personally trained them to be his own elite force, different from the scum that made up the rest of his organization. He had managed to find ten such cases, among whom Os was the third oldest.

None of his chosen few knew why Vyrga had trained them instead of normal children. Maybe the reason was empathy for kindred spirits, or maybe it was pragmatism on the off chance that he could establish connections with some nobles. What they did understand was that Vyrga saw no difference between a powerful chief and a crippled beggar. For Vyrga, life was life, and the end of all life was death. In any case, almost all of the ten chosen were thankful for his care. Almost all of them...

"You were right. Gelmar is a traitor," reported Os.

"Figures," spat Vyrga in disdain. He had known from Gelmar's childhood that Gelmar could not be trusted, yet he had wished that he was wrong, as Gelmar had been the first child to follow him. To Vyrga, Gelmar was, or rather had been, both a son and a friend.

"Why is he doing this, though? Why does he want to take over?"

"Don't fool yourself, Os." Vyrga flipped his flute over and ran his fingers down its body. "We all know Gelmar's power-hungry. It didn't sit well with him that you and Heimo are more likely to succeed me. But unlike Ludger and Bolo, he doesn't respect me enough to wait until I die before setting his plan in motion. He wants everything for himself, right now."

"Wait... what? Ludger and Bolo want to take over as well?"

"No, those two spoke to me earlier. They told me that if anything happens to me, they'll leave and form their own gang. Ludger doesn't find you fit to be my replacement, and we both know that Bolo is always following behind his older brother. You and Ludger have always competed to be my second-in-command, and he's got you basically matched in terms of skill and competence, which makes him justifiably unsatisfied with the decision."

"If we're basically matched, why did you choose me?"

"Because you're the cool-headed one. Ludger has quite the temper."

Os was not too convinced that that was the only reason. In his experience, he knew that there were times when a passionate leader like Ludger, who could inspire his men to march through hell, would prove more valuable than a calm, thoughtful leader like himself.

Vyrga looked up from his flute. "And between you and me, I get along with you more."

"I... see," Os replied, half grateful and half disappointed. Though he appreciated that Vyrga favoured him, it did not feel right that favouritism had tipped the balance.

Os felt strangely obligated to speak up for Ludger, but Vyrga preempted his protest. "Ludger knows the true reason and he has no problem with it. He knows that you're closer to me and my ideals than he or any of the others will be, and he doesn't hate you for it."

"But boss, does he hate you?"

"Probably not." Vyrga shrugged. "Os, do you know why I kept teaching you all that the world is unfair, unruly, and unkind? I want you all to accomplish great things without the chains of laws, morals, society, the gods, or a traitorous idiot who thinks he's smart enough to use your own philosophy against you," he emphasised.

"Oh, right. What'll we do about Gelmar?"

"Remember when I told you to send the deserter's head to the fledgling?"

"To Gherm? Yes, yes I did. That wasn't just a warning, right? Don't you think using Pog like that was a bit... extreme?"

"To answer your first question, no, it *was* a mere warning, but not for the reason you think. It was to rile the fledgling up before testing him."

Os' eyes widened. "You're going to send Gelmar to attack him."

"Yup." Vyrga nonchalantly placed his flute off to the side. "I've heard about how he's training his men, and believe me, he's not training them to play lord of the slums—he's training an army. He's as ambitious as I am."

"And if he fails?"

"Then he'll be proven worthless. Would be a shame, really. Not too many folks in our world who can stand up to corruption."

Os nodded. "If you say so. But again, wasn't punishing Pog like that too extreme?"

"For a deserter? Not really. People like that agree to commit all sorts of crimes and atrocities when it's convenient for them, but when they've reached their limit, they think they can wash their hands of it all just like that. They excuse their actions by saying that they had no other choice, even though I never told them to kill and rape. I actually don't like enabling those kinds of activities."

"Yet... you don't stop them. No offence, boss, but that's hypocrisy."

"It is, but if I had to stop every sadistic idiot who does the first thing on his mind, we'd never have grown this big. Besides, infamy has its uses. It gets these scum in line. And we won't keep them forever—they'll be purged as fodder when it's time to break our shackles."

"But what about the kids? Since when do we kill *kids*?"

Vyrga hesitated. "We don't. I left the task of killing the lout to Gelmar and he took it too far," he said with a tinge of regret. "Thankfully, Bolo managed to save the wife and daughter and sneak them out of our territory with some extra merits added to their records, which is better than leaving them there. Considering those kids were already dead, well, I did approve the use of their heads."

"That's horrible—"

"It is, but we do what we need to do. We have our entire lives to regret our actions." Vyrga sighed again. "Right now it's time to call Gelmar. Tell him to gather his men and prepare to attack."

"Alright, boss." Os turned to leave the room.

"Oh, one more thing."

"Yes?"

"There's a "parcel" that we need to deliver to one of our noble *customers.* Remind the courier that we only accept payment in coins, not merits."

"Shouldn't all our couriers know this by now? They've all accompanied us on our visits to the pigs above."

"This courier is new, and this will be his first assignment. If he fails, it'll be his last," Vyrga said with a sneer.

"As requested. Anything else?"

"No, on your way."

"Will do," he replied before leaving the room

Vyrga was alone again at last. He gingerly picked his flute back up and raised it to his lips. *Don't disappoint me, Gherm. If that's who you really are,* he thought before playing his sad tune once again.

CHAPTER 10

GREY ANGST

Silence.

Silence enveloped the area as the gathered bogeys stood at attention. The gathering of these newly-organized vagrants fell under the command of one greyborn, Gelmar.

Few would ever have expected such discipline from this bunch of lowlifes. They were more known as the scourge of the rest of the Vyrga's men, constituting the largest party under his banner. It also comprised the vilest criminals of them all.

However, all sixty-four of them now looked as tame as puppies for one reason alone: to avoid their leader's wrath.

Gelmar was livid. Not only had Vyrga chosen someone else to succeed him, but also he now had given Gelmar orders to put down a runt—not just any runt, but a runt commanding enough troops to threaten Gelmar's numbers. Against a single naysayer, or even a small gathering of them, there would be no problem, but against a force as large as half of Gelmar's own? It was obvious Vyrga was culling Gelmar's numbers to crush even the possibility of a coup.

"Gelm!" called a voice, startling all the vagrants. There was only one individual who could get away with addressing their commander by that nickname: Heimo, Gelmar's closest friend.

"Heimo... What do you want?" Gelmar said coldly to the second youngest of Vyrga's elites.

"Why are you treating me like this, Gelm?" Heimo protested, indignant. "You know it wasn't my choice. I don't even want to be

Vyrga's successor."

"But he still chose you over me!" Gelmar retorted. "And you know what's worse? Os! He chose Os, too!"

"Bro, calm down—"

"Don't you 'bro' me! We were never brothers! You were just another wretch that Vyrga picked up, who turned around and took what was supposed to be mine! I hate you!" Gelmar yelled, shocking both his men and Heimo. Gelmar had never treated him this way, and from Heimo's expression, it was easy to see that he was hurt.

"I-I just wanted to make sure you stayed safe."

"Why? Do you think I'm that useless, mister genius? I'm just going to put down a runt. Isn't that right, boys!" he yelled at his men. He received no response; they were still shocked at his behavior. They had never seen him act so heartless towards Heimo. Towards others? Sure, but not Heimo.

"I said, *isn't that right, boys!*" he roared with a murderous glint in his eyes.

"Y-Yeah!" they yelled back out of sync, causing Gelmar's left eye to twitch.

He turned his attention back to Heimo. "See? We're ready to squash that bug!"

Heimo grimaced. "Don't underestimate him. This Gherm isn't a 'bug'—he's managed to build a force despite having only two kills to his name. And from what my spies managed to pass on, although his men consist of regular miners and other usual targets, he's been training them for much more than skirmishes. Training your men to use spears and shields is normal, but training all your men on how to stand and walk in certain positions and use slings is not!" Heimo valued Gelmar dearly, but did not want Gelmar's men to see him vulnerable the way only Gelmar had. "There's something not right about him. Even if you don't care for me as a brother, I beg of you, watch out."

Gelmar sighed. As ashamed at his actions as he was, it did not feel right to apologize to Heimo, for he had already tarnished their bond. "I know about the slings and the training. Vyrga told me. Look at our equipment."

Heimo turned around and saw that all of Gelmar's men were wearing wooden helmets and wielding small, round wooden shields. The shields looked too crude to last more than a few shots, and the helmets could only be described as shabby and hastily produced. Heimo said nothing.

"What? We were only informed a few hours ago! Besides, we're double their numbers. I heard they're only thirty-three strong."

"That intel is a week late! We don't know how many more men he's gathered under his command and what tricks he's hiding from us. You can't just go like this."

"What do you expect me to do! That piece of shit is forcing us to go!" countered Gelmar.

"That bogey you're calling a piece of shit *raised* us!" Heimo yelled back. He could tolerate being humiliated by Gelmar, but not hearing Gelmar or anybody else insult their benefactor. If it had not been for Vyrga, Heimo would have been a broken mess a long time ago.

"He's using us, just like everybody else!"

"We *chose* to follow him!"

"You're a dog like the rest of them!"

"Do you even know what a dog is?"

Gelmar was flustered. If he were to answer honestly, he had never seen one in his entire life. "It's..." He quickly turned the question around. "Do you?"

Now it was Heimo's turn to be flustered. Only a few greyborns had ever seen an actual dog, and he was not one of them. Even Vyrga had only glimpsed one by chance when some supposedly important noble had secretly visited him to cut a deal. Heimo could only repeat Vyrga's description to answer Gelmar. "It's a... giant domesticated fox."

"A fox? Like those creatures in the underground forest?" Gelmar was unsure which idea confused him more: that those things called "foxes" could be tamed, or that a dog was something similar.

"Y-Yes... Those."

After a while of awkward silence, one of Gelmar's men decided to save both Heimo and Gelmar from further embarrassment. "Um... Boss. The men are ready."

Gelmar's spirits were lifted instantly. "Great! Alright, boys, time to squash some bugs. We only have ten days before the expedition, so let's finish this early. Are you ready?"

"Yeah!" his men screamed with vigour. Finally, they could kill and plunder to their hearts' content.

Heimo showed Gelmar a wry expression. "You're not taking this seriously, are you?"

"Despite what you and Vyrga think, Heimo, I'm not stupid. I'll send a few scouts beforehand to avoid any nasty surprises. I won't let some pipsqueak with a silver tongue destroy my dream."

"Your dream? You really think you can accomplish that?" Heimo knew exactly what Gelmar wished for, and knew even better just how impossible it would be even for someone like Vyrga, let alone Gelmar, to achieve it. Many greater bogeys, goblins, and members of other species had tried and failed to reach the prominence of the Enlightened One.

"As always, you think I'm delusional."

"The 'Enlightened One' is a myth, Gelmar. Do you really believe that there was once a goblin who conquered all the people of the forest and established a great clan consisting of hundreds of tribes of bogeys, goblins, kobolds, tree people, cat people, and all the other species?"

"Who knows what's possible under great leadership?"

Heimo rolled his eyes. "And how about the part where the 'Enlightened One' made large bronze cauldrons that could shoot thunder and lead balls? Or the part when he and his inner court made iron stronger than bronze—stronger than bronze! *Iron!*"

"Many mysteries were lost through time," Gelmar said, stubbornly folding his arms.

"And what about the part where he mysteriously grows stronger and changes his form every few battles? And I'm not talking about putting on muscle after constant physical exertion—I mean when he suddenly doubles in size in under an hour! And that part where he grants that ability to his subordinates—I call that bullshit! Creatures, with the exception of insects, cannot change form like that!"

"We've both seen goblins, Heimo. How can you explain how some rare ones have horns and others have red skin or some other weird colour?"

"Easy, birth defects. I've once seen a bogey born with six fingers on each hand."

"That doesn't sound like a defect to me. I thought you were smarter than that."

"You know what I mean!"

"Heh, I know. Non-believer."

Heimo frowned and rubbed his forehead. "If Ainshart the Great, also known as the 'Enlightened One,' was real, can you please explain to me, *where did all that progress go?* How did all those marvellous tools and wondrous magic disappear? And why has nobody recreated them?"

"Another easy question. After he was poisoned by his own children, they mobilized their respective factions against each other and fought until almost nothing was left. Each leader destroyed all those innovations because they didn't want their rivals to get them.

"The reason nobody has rediscovered the artifacts is that Ainshart's blessing, which increased both our leaders' strength and our collective intelligence, has run out. That's right, Heimo. As we speak, the entire goblinoid evolutionary tree is collectively getting dumber and dumber. And let's not forget that we goblinoids keep warring nonstop with other races, so there isn't even any time to rediscover those old secrets. Also, non-believer shits like you keep us all in the dark."

"I see you've taken to repeating the same spiel those religious nuts give every time someone questions them."

"Well most bogeys *are* believers, and all of us speak the Enlightened One's language. Heck, most of us, even you, are named in this language. The only bogeys I know named using the old tongue are Vyrga, that Rak guy, and my target, Gherm. Speaking of him, it's time to go." Gelmar gruffly turned his back to Heimo and began to march to the front of his men, stopping midway to briefly let go of his pride and say what he truly wanted to say. "And I'm sorry, bro. I was a little too pissed off."

Heimo chuckled in surprise. "Heh. No worries, bro. Just take care of yourself, and don't lose." He inflected as much hope as he could into that last request.

"I won't. See you soon," Gelmar said with a grin before leading his men to battle. There was, after all, blood to be spilt.

CHAPTER II
THIS MEANS WAR

Two hours had passed before Gelmar could make out Gherm's encampment in the distance at the very edge of Rak's sphere of influence. Pockets of light trickling down from a few holes in the tunnel ceiling fed the patches of moss creeping ever closer to the middle of the path.

Gelmar and his men set up camp. An hour later, his scouts returned with intelligence about Gherm's forces: they numbered about twenty men, and there were no obvious traps in sight. Gherm and his men had erected two barricades consisting of whatever wooden objects they could find, mostly sharpened wooden boards and tables with bags of cave dirt propping up the stakes. One barricade was visible with the naked eye from Gelmar's camp, but the other was some distance away, nestled tightly in a residential area.

The scouts had also snuck peeks inside whatever homes they could, where they found unarmed women, youths, and elders hiding from the conflict, but no evidence of an ambush.

"Looks like they've been expecting us," Gelmar mused.

"Looks like it, boss," cut in a scout, eager to be acknowledged. "They're just a bunch of kivvigs between us now."

"Did I ask? And it's *killigs*, not 'kivvigs.'"

"Um... What do killigs even mean?" The flustered thug asked.

"Really? You've gone your whole *life* not knowing what a killig is?"

"Sorry, boss."

"You should be. To keep it short, Killigs were an order of great holy warriors who guarded Ainshart's throne room. They were all the same height, twice that of a goblin, so people eventually measured things relative to their height."

"So where are they now and why aren't there more of their race?"

Gelmar frowned. "You were around since the last expedition, right? So you've seen their race."

"I did? There wasn't anyone except us, the upper bastards, the nobles, and the goblins, right?"

"Right. And they were goblins."

His answer made his followers speechless, but then the scout broke from his stupor and asked, "How?"

Gelmar smiled "A thorough process of selective breeding and the use of one of Ainshart's greatest miracles, the ability to change a lifeform and make it stronger. And before you ask, Hos can mean either toes or feet depending on dialect, but we tend to use it to judge things foot sized so you can guess what we interpret it as. Now that we're done wasting our time with trivia, do you have anything actually useful to say?"

"Sorry, boss, I got nothing. But something isn't right about them."

"They should've numbered at least thirty-three."

"Yeah! Where the heck are the others?"

Gelmar shrugged. "Either they ran away once they heard we were coming, or they're hiding in the nearby vicinity. But we've already searched the vicinity, so it *has* to be the first option. Damned cowards."

"Boss!" another voice yelled. Gelmar spotted a few troops from the rear guard running towards him.

"B-Boss, it's—"

Gelmar threw a hand up, and instantly the guard stopped talking. "Don't tell me. Vyrga's on our tails?"

"H-How did you—"

"It's obvious. If we disobeyed him or failed to kill Gherm, he wouldn't hesitate to kill us himself."

"You don't mean—"

"Our coup is an open secret, dumbass! The only thing that Vyrga lacks is proof. He might play scoundrel, but he still won't kill his own without a reason. If we win, some of us will die, but he won't do a thing. If we lose or run away, he'll take care of us himself."

The guard tilted his head thoughtfully. "In that case, why not join this Gherm?"

"Great idea. If we combine forces, we'll be about eighty men, and we'd just need to fight more than three hundred other men with better equipment and better leaders." His voice steadily increased in volume. "Why not die with them, right? We'll be remembered as traitors together!" he barked, spittle collecting on the cowering underling's face.

The rest of his troops lowered their heads as fear took root in their hearts.

"Why the long faces? Don't tell me you believe that we'll lose to some unknown runt and a measly twenty men!" Gelmar yelled, catching their attention. "Have you forgotten who you are? Who *we* are? We're the bane of all greyborns! We're the monsters that cause men to cry! Whenever our enemies hear my name, they lose all hope! For I am Gelmar, and you all are my warriors. All we have to do is squish some bugs and Vyrga won't be able to do shit! Are you all actually worried we'll lose to some newcomer and his band of day-labourers?"

"No!" they yelled with fervour.

"Are we going to take what's theirs? Remind everyone why we are feared?"

"Yes!" his men replied with glee. They loved a good pillage after spilling some blood—what could twenty-one bogeys possibly do?

Gelmar and his army proceeded to the tunnel to face Gherm. Five of Gherm's troops were lined up side-by-side in the front, their broad, rectangular wooden shields in hand ready to block invaders and short spears to stab anyone left. Another five followed behind them wielding longer spears with harder points. The remaining ten formed the back line, slings in hand, ready to fire their projectiles at all invaders who came into their sight, and in the middle of the armed force stood the tiny bogey Gherm wearing a wooden helmet and proudly brandishing his spear.

Gherm and his army were positioned behind a shoddy wooden barricade and in front of a sturdier barricade a short hundred killigs behind the slingers. Gelmar's men wielded a variety of weapons ranging from stone knives to wooden clubs. Gelmar himself wielded a copper-headed axe, bestowed upon him by Vyrga as a gift for his contribution in a former battle. Gelmar commanded sixty-four men in total.

Gelmar surveyed the area for anything that could affect the battle. There were stalagmites covered in cloth, whose purpose he could not discern, every few hundred killigs between his encampment and the front line of Gherm's formation. Quadrupedal corpse-eaters slunk up the walls and gathered en masse upon the numerous stalactites above them, their black scales glinting in the faint trickles of sunlight and their yellow eyes anticipating the feast soon to come.

Questions raced rapid-fire through Gelmar's head. *A shield wall? Why attempt such a thing with so few men? And why two layers of fortifications? Once we break through the wooden barrier and the shield wall, there won't be enough time for them to retreat behind the second one,* he pondered.

Bogeys have decent night vision—why are his men carrying so many torches? He focused more intently on the row of shields behind the front row, upon each of which was painted a red eye, the symbol of the goddess of war. *Why are the shields almost all covered in that... yellowish stuff?*

The questions kept echoing in Gelmar's mind as he walked to meet Gherm before the start of the battle. This was a custom of bogey-kind: before two forces of bogeys began to fight, their leaders either negotiated for peace or waged a war of words before the war of weapons. Every bogey, from the highest of nobles to the lowest of thugs, followed this custom. Usually, the two belligerents would have a priest mediate the conflict, but Gelmar was under no illusion that they could possibly find a priest in this blighted place, and why would he want anything other than to win in combat against this no-name runt?

Gelmar at last came face-to-face with Gherm at the centre of the battlefield. Gelmar glared at his adversary; Gherm replied with a smirk.

Gelmar was quick to initiate. "*You're* Gherm? Hah! I thought it'd be someone impressive, not an actual runt!" he boomed loudly enough for all to hear.

"I prefer to be called Lev," returned his counterpart nonchalantly. "And you are?"

"'Lev?' What kind of name is that? And you honestly don't know who I am? The name's Gelmar, and I'll be your death!"

"Pfft... Hahaha! Was that supposed to be threatening? And— oh. Gelmar? Thank goodness. I thought Vyrga would send us one of the good ones."

Gelmar's jaws clenched. Lev resumed his diatribe.

"It's true, you're second-rate— wait, no, make that third-rate material. Your men are undisciplined trash who only obey orders out of fear, and we all know *you* just want Vyrga to acknowledge you." Lev smugly watched Gelmar foam at the mouth. "Meh, you'll do. My men do need some practice after all."

Gelmar was livid. As much as he wanted to tear this arrogant bastard limb from limb, he had to restrain himself. *I may serve Vyrga, but I would never stoop that low,* he thought.

Instead, Gelmar stepped forward, invading Lev's personal space until Lev craned his neck to maintain eye contact. "You know what? Once we slaughter your men, I won't kill you. I'll just make your life a living hell. I'm going to take everything and everyone you value and break them slowly. Your neighbours? They'll hate you. Your sister? She'll abandon you. Whatever spawn she'll have from my men? They'll curse you! All those who believed in you, all those who put their trust in you, all those who ever cared about you? They'll wither away wishing you'd burn forever and ever in damnation for turning their life into hell, for pissing me off."

Lev's smile disappeared. Gelmar thought he had claimed a verbal victory, but when he looked into Lev's eyes, he saw no fear. Instead, he saw an emptiness that threatened to devour him whole.

"You know," said Lev in a voice so cold that Gelmar felt a chill on his nape, "usually I can tolerate pointless drivel from wannabe edgelords like you, but you just had to try too hard, didn't you? It was okay when you threatened me with death. Many others have done the same, but none, except one," he chuckled cryptically, "have delivered."

Except one? thought Gelmar.

Lev continued, another dastardly smile creeping up his face. "But you just had to threaten my friends, didn't you? Let me tell you, the things I care about can be counted on one hand, and I'll allow nothing to harm them. Not you. Not Vyrga. Not Rak. Not the nobles, not the goblins, not the gods."

"That's blasphemy!" Gelmar replied, his voice cracking.

With conviction that could have made the ender serpent cower in fear, Lev spoke again. "That is the truth." His eyes narrowed. "Now run along and pray for forgiveness from whatever being you believe in, because trust me, you won't be getting any from me."

Lev returned to his men, seemingly melting into a wall of impassioned cheers. Gelmar heard shuffling and hushed whispers from his own side.

"Are you okay, boss?" asked one of Gelmar's henchmen upon his boss's return.

"I'm fine," he began, color returning to his face. "As dangerous as he seems, threats are nothing but words until proven otherwise." *And getting shaken before the battle won't help at all,* he reminded himself. He closed his eyes and recalled why he needed to win: Vyrga would put his whole army to death if they lost. And they would definitely win.

Gelmar turned to his men, and the whispers and shuffling came to a halt. "Prepare to attack! Kill them all! Let's bring that bastard's head home on a spike!"

His men erupted in a unified cheer before brandishing their weapons and awaiting his signal.

Raising a fist into the air, Gelmar roared, "Kill them all!" His men sped forward.

* * *

"What did you say to him, sir?" Volker asked Lev immediately as he returned to the barricade. Before Lev had faced Gelmar, Volker had ordered the men to cover the barricade with as much dried moss as they could find and position the barrels in front of the shield bearers. Presently, Lev was inspecting the barricade, his protégé in tow.

"Nothing," Lev replied, "I just riled him up."

"If I may, sir, that didn't look like 'nothing' to me."

Lev shrugged. "It's always good to piss off idiots. It makes it easier for them to blunder."

"Oh, that explains the rage, but why the fear?"

Lev hesitated. "To demoralize his men?"

"But wouldn't that make them more cautious? What if they discover our—"

"Sir! They've started the attack!" screamed a shield bearer as he saw Gelmar and his men begin their charge.

"We'll continue the discussion later, Volker. Everyone, get into formation!" Lev shouted, relieved he did not need to explain himself right then. "Shield bearers, block the path! Spearmen, prepare yourselves! Slingers, load projectiles!"

"Sir, yes, sir!" His shield bearers tightened their formation. Their mighty shields slammed on the ground, ready to block the path of their foes.

Lev had observed that his three-man formation was viable against single opponents of greater physical strength, including hivelings, and even small squads of enemies. However, it could never work against Vyrga's men once they had consolidated into an army whose number either equalled or exceeded Lev's.

Accordingly, Lev had refocused training his men on discipline, formations, and spear thrusting. Cognizant of how little time he had, he had trained them to form a shield wall, a combat tactic that was both easy to teach them and a sizable morale boost. Even impromptu combatants could summon bravery if they were standing shoulder-to-shoulder with their comrades.

Lev, likewise, knew that the shield formation had many disadvantages. The formation was susceptible to flanks, and would eventually weaken over time under constant ranged pressure. Once breached, the defensive line was almost impossible to re-establish. Despite its flaws, though, Lev was quite sure he could secure victory with the bag of tricks he had at his disposal.

"W-Will we be alright, sir?" Volker asked, his voice barely above a whisper.

Gelmar and his men pressed forward, passing the first stalagmite. Their thundering footsteps and madness-filled laughter echoed within the cavern and clashed with the terrified babbling from Lev's men.

"Is this plan going to work?"

"Why am I even here? What's gotten into me?"

"Mother, I'm sorry!"

Unlike Gelmar, Lev's men were simple miners and labourers, most of them youths who had neither gone on an expedition nor ever killed anything larger than a rat or a lizard. They were not warriors accustomed to fighting, let alone killing—they were simple folk who wanted to lead simple lives, and that was what Lev had used to inspire them.

"Are you afraid?" Lev yelled.

His men lowered their heads in shame.

"So am I," he continued at an almost pensive, but still audible, volume. "But I'm more afraid of losing. For if we lose, we won't just lose our lives—those bastards will target our parents, our siblings, our wives, and our children! But I won't allow it. Neither," he said, his voice climbing in volume again, "should *you*! We always get trampled on by their ilk! We always suffer at the hands of such scoundrels and never dare to fight back! No matter how much we beg, they never show mercy. They never stop harming those we love."

Perfect, they're paying attention now, he discerned. *But Gelmar's fast. I should wrap this up.*

"For once we will not leave ourselves at their mercy! We *will* protect our homes! We *will* protect our families! We *will win*!"

"We will *win!*" his men repeated with vigour. With every chant, their voices came to harmonize in synchronicity. They planted their feet firmly to face the approaching horde head-on.

Just as the enemies reached the second stalagmite, the slingers launched their attack.

More than ten leaden projectiles of varying shapes and sizes flew into the air before slamming into the shields and bodies of Gelmar's men. *Just as I'd planned,* Lev mused, *the short distance and the narrowness of this tunnel make it really hard to miss.*

Already six of Gelmar's men had been hit, two of them fatally. One had sustained a small round bullet to his forehead, killing him instantly, while another took a larger acorn-shaped shot to his stomach, knocking him to the ground seconds before the rest of his oblivious allies trampled him.

Yet neither their fallen ally nor the onslaught of projectiles stopped Gelmar and his men from pressing forward. By the time they finally reached the last stalagmite, they had lost ten soldiers, but only Gelmar seemed hesitant to touch the barrier. A few of his men, meanwhile, had begun to scale the barricade.

Is Gelmar the only one noticing the casualties? Lev wondered. "Shield bearers! Push the barrels!"

As commanded, the shield bearers removed the barrels' lids and knocked the barrels over with their shields. A dark brown, viscous liquid spilled onto and covered both the wooden barricade and the moss beneath it.

"Spearmen! Shield bearers! Retreat to the second line!" The invaders approaching, Lev raised a nearby torch with a flourish, then chucked the still-lit torch onto the barricade, which instantaneously erupted into flames. "Hope you like tar," he muttered.

He turned to the slingers. "Let's leave them a little surprise, shall we!"

Lev dashed away from the crackling wall.

Gelmar wrinkled his nose at the slingers abandoning their position to run away with the rest of Lev's troops. *Why now?* he thought.

He soon received his answer. Suddenly, cries of shock and pain from Gelmar's more brazen bogeys filled the air. In their race to scale the barricade, the dark liquid had smeared on their arms and legs. In seconds, this liquid caught fire, burning their limbs. Though they waved their arms and dashed about, screaming in agony, the burning tar continued to eat through their flesh.

Gelmar and the rest of his men halted. The billowing smoke from the barricade blocked their sight, to say nothing of the literal wall of fire between them and their quarry.

"Boss! Vyrga's here!" yelled a man in the back.

Gelmar looked backwards. Where he had delivered his speech before the battle, Vyrga now stood, accompanied by Os, Ludger, and a hundred loyal men, weapons brandished. Gelmar cursed under his breath.

Panic swept over his men. They understood what Vyrga's presence meant. If they retreated, Vyrga would put them to death. If they waited for the fire to die out, Lev would escape, and Vyrga would still put them to death. And if they forced their way forward, many of them would burn to death. They were trapped.

Gelmar's eyes darted from floor to ceiling, far to near, shack to house to shack. "Men! Raid the houses! Get as much water as you can!"

Screams erupted from within as Gelmar's men forced their way inside.

Gelmar's mob lugged barrels of water back to the barricade and flung their contents onto the burning wood, quelling the flames.

Gelmar raised his axe high. "These are miners we're fighting! Kill 'em all!" he roared.

The men roared in reciprocity. To them, this was not a battle; it was a farce, but not in the way they had hoped. They had been injured, tricked, and humiliated by a mere twenty-one weaklings who had never before set foot on a battlefield. Even if they annihilated their targets now, the humiliation afterwards would still be unavoidable. Thirteen of them had died and they had yet to score a single kill! Against miners!

Gelmar's men, what was left of them, finally recommenced their charge as they climbed over the still-hot wood and dropped down onto the other side.

There they saw their enemy once more behind the second, sturdier barricade, but in a new formation. The shield wall blocked the path, which had yet again narrowed, effectively allowing no openings in the front line. Spears were extended over the shields, ready to impale all those who approached. Slingers stood in the back with their loaded slings, ready to rain death on their enemies once more. It was the exact formation as before, except there were no barrels beside the barricade.

The expressions on the faces of Gelmar's men collectively transitioned from shock, to confusion, to fear, and finally to glee. Behind Lev's men were Rak's, but rather than serving as backup, Rak's party blocked Lev's path of retreat.

Gelmar drew a striking conclusion: if Lev's army tried to retreat, they, too, would face death. Gelmar cackled gleefully.

"Um... Couldn't this be a trap, boss?" asked one of his more cautious fighters.

"Hah! You don't know Rak as well as I do. Out of everything in this world, he hates spineless weaklings the most," replied Gelmar confidently. From what he remembered, Rak had accompanied Vyrga many times and met many nobles who had like war-chiefs but cowered like corpse-eaters when the going got tough. "He's testing 'Lev' to see whether he's worth keeping around," Gelmar continued.

"'Lev'?" asked the fighter, confused.

"That's what Gherm is calling himself. More importantly, now that we know the truth," said Gelmar emphatically, "what do you say we do?"

"Tear 'em apart! Kill 'em all!" clamored his men.

"Good! Kill them all!" Gelmar roared, rushing towards his adversaries.

"Kill! Kill! Kill!" his men chanted as they followed his orders. Some rushed ahead of Gelmar to eager to prove themselves on the field of combat.

Once again, Lev's slingers launched their lead bullets. In response, Gelmar and his band raised their shields above them mid-charge. Missile after missile slammed into their shields, but only two bogeys fell.. The first lost the upper half of his already-worn shield to a round shot before taking an oblong shot to the throat. The second took an acorn-shaped bullet to his knee, causing him to fall and smash his face on a jagged rock.

Gelmar grinned. The losses were a setback, but his men were making ground.

"Aaaah!"

"Owww!"

"What the— Aaack!"

Gelmar's grin vanished as the air filled with screams of pain, including his own. Something had punctured the sole of his right foot, almost causing him to drop his shield, and jerked his foot upwards with a start.

An obstacle with four spikes arranged tetrahedrally—a caltrop—had embedded itself into his sweating, bleeding foot.

In merciless succession, a lead ball slammed into the base of his shield. Gelmar lost his balance, stepping on another caltrop behind him, and howled in pain again.

The battlefield was filled with the wails of Gelmar's men as they suffered from both the rain of lead and the spikes on the ground. They desperately raised and held their shields above their heads, but another five men promptly fell to the bombardment, and their corpses littered the ground.

Gelmar gritted his teeth as he removed the caltrops from his feet. In a display of resilience, he continued moving forward and called out to his men, "Don't let some petty tricks stop you!" He pointed his axe ahead. "We're halfway there! They can't keep this up forever!" The field of caltrops ended a mere twenty killigs ahead.

Their courage bolstered somewhat, Gelmar's men determinedly continued forward, albeit at a slower pace as they tried to avoid stepping on the damned torture devices. Their bodies were covered in sweat, bruises, and still-bleeding lacerations, their minds were weary from all the losses and surprises that had happened in this joke of a battle.

But there remained a single thought in their minds, the sole force driving them forward: *revenge*. Gone were the expectations of an easy victory; gone were the souls of their companions whose bodies now littered the entire living quarters from start to end. Gelmar and his men wanted to crush Lev more than anything in the world. They wanted to tear those who now taunted and mocked them limb from limb. They wanted to make Lev's men suffer as they had suffered and nothing more.

Step by step, they growled and cursed as they navigated through the dreadful terrain.

Step by step, their hatred for Lev and his men increased as more lead bullets managed to claim the lives of their comrades. By the time they had gotten past the field of caltrops, another five men had been lost.

As the distance between the two sides closed with less than a hundred killigs between them, Gelmar could see the panic on the faces of his enemies. Along with blood, sweat and piss, he could smell their fear, though he could not deduce why until the rain of lead slowed to a trickle and eventually stopped entirely.

"They ran out of lead," an observer whispered.

And he was right. The slingers launched their missiles once more, but this time they launched stones.

Gelmar's mob picked up the pace, hoping to break the shield wall and slaughter the men behind them, hoping to end it all and finally drop the curtains on this accursed, bloody play once and for all.

Voooooh! The ear-splitting sound of a horn pierced the battlefield.

CHAPTER 12

DAWN

"Ambush!" yelled Gotthard in a panic.

A small bullet whistled through the air, slamming into the back of the man's head from one of the nearby houses that they passed through, penetrating his skull and killing him instantly.

"Break into the houses and kill those sons of bitches!" snarled Gelmar. Few of his men heard his command above the shrill sounds of the projectiles; those who did charged towards the houses, only to be met with javelins thrown out the windows. Some managed to back away, some blocked the flying spears with their shields, while some were skewered without knowing what was going on.

Even then, Gelmar's men doggedly tried to push their way into the houses, only to find the entrances blocked with large rectangular shields covered in yellowish-white sap with a red eye drawn in the centres. Gelmar's men tried to bash through, but the shields absorbed the impact from their weapons.

Gelmar caught a whiff of the shields—they smelled unusually pungent. Gelmar concluded that they were covered with the sap of bluecatcher mushrooms, a giant, blue, luminescent, carnivorous species found on the second layer and lower, which used its sticky sap to catch prey before encapsulating it for digestion. Their sap worked well as adhesive for wood, leather, and cloth—he was loath to admit that it worked just as well in sticking the stone of his men's weapons to the shields.

The men wavered. Not only had they played into another scheme of their enemies, but their numbers were not that much greater than those of their enemies. The only advantage Gelmar's men had left was that they were more experienced in combat, but that was meaningless if they couldn't reach their targets.

Projectiles assaulting them from all sides, Gelmar's men huddled together, shields raised, and formed a shield wall of their own. Because their shields were smaller, their wall was not as effective as Lev's, but it managed to protect them from most of the shots.

"Huddle closer and charge!" shouted Gelmar, intending to overlap the shields into a tight shell. His men obediently huddled closer, but before they could charge forward, something fell on top of them, tangling them together.

"Nets?" Gelmar exclaimed. He peeked through a gap in the shield shell to find women, children, and a couple of elders glaring down at them with seething hate. He could not place them, but some of them looked familiar.

"Hey... Isn't that Pog's wife?" yelled Gotthard, tangled with him. *Pog... That's right, he had a wife and kids,* Gelmar realized. *Are they all... families of those we've killed—*

"B-Boss! Look!" interrupted another soldier, pointing to their back where bogeys holding spears, shields, and slings were walking out of their houses, grouping into the same formation as the ones before them.

Gelmar sharply inhaled. "Cut the nets!" he screamed.

The first formation left their barricade and began its approach, followed by the second formation. Gelmar's men, ignoring the unceasing onslaught of rocks and bullets, the pain from their wounds, and the unmoving bodies of those who had fallen before them, managed to cut themselves free. They immediately stood up and raised their weapons in defiance.

Now the real battle had begun—Lev and his forty-odd men against

Gelmar and his remaining thirty-five.

Gelmar's forces charged at the first formation with all their remaining strength at once, hoping to break through and finish off Lev to throw their enemy into disarray.

As he and his men charged forward, Gelmar saw Lev flinch before yelling further orders at his men.

The shield walls, along with the rest of Lev's men, moved backwards to put more space between themselves and Gelmar, but Gelmar's mob maintained their pace.

Lev then pulled out his horn and blew on it two times. The slingers stopped firing, moved closer to the shield wall, and threw some bags in the air.

Gelmar watched the bags fall to the ground and burst open, spreading caltrops on the floor.

"Not this again! Spikes!" he yelled. His men halted their advance, much to his chagrin. "Who told you to stop? Just avoid them or push them out of the way!"

Gelmar's men continued forth as fast as they could, avoiding the caltrops. Most, but not all, managed to either avoid them or sweep them out of their way, though Gelmar's men had to move in haste to stay ahead of the formation in the rear.

Once they passed through the field of caltrops, Lev's slingers shrank behind their barricade once more, while Gelmar's troops quickened their pace against the perspiring protests of their muscles. Their eyes shone with vigour, and they filled the air with defiant roars as they crashed into the now-shaking wall.

The shield-bearer in the middle, a simple-looking kid, and the spearman behind him leaped out of the way to the sides, creating a gap in the formation. From that gap, Gelmar's men could see Lev a stone's throw away.

"Hahahahaha! The cowards couldn't keep the line together!" laughed Gelmar before his expression hardened. "Ignore the rest and get that runt!" Gelmar himself forced his way through the gap and darted towards the fleeing Lev.

Gelmar chased after him. The shield bearers and spearmen stood in place. The slingers retreated into the nearby houses. None of these moves made strategic sense to Gelmar, but he did not need them to make sense. He only needed Lev's head.

With Lev's head, Gelmar was certain Vyrga would spare him.

Lev came dangerously close to Rak's men, who had their weapons raised to cut him down. With Gelmar in hot pursuit, Lev swiftly pivoted to the left and slipped through a doorway, and naturally, Gelmar followed him inside to a dark room.

While Gelmar took a moment for his eyes to adjust to the decreased light level, he felt danger incoming. He instinctively ducked, narrowly dodging a spear Lev had aimed at his head.

"You son of a— *Aghhh*!" he exclaimed as a clay bowl smashed into his face. He heard Lev run into the next room.

"What... happened... boss?" breathed Gotthard, sweat dripping down his forehead. He, too, had barely managed to keep up.

"*After him!*" Gelmar snarled, running into the next room. The room was empty save for a gently drafty window.

Gelmar rushed to the window and found Lev running to another house further ahead across the alley. Gelmar vaulted over the windowsill.

Slipping in and out of empty houses, the two commanders continued to play cat and mouse, costing Gelmar two more of his soldiers. One died after Lev threw a knife into his throat, while the other, having tried to grab Lev, found his neck snapped in half. As for the bogeys who had been foolish enough to wait outside windows, Lev dispatched them by throwing a table out the windows first, then using the fallen table as a ledge to leap to safety.

As Gelmar approached the door of the sixth house, his muscles screamed for the air that his lungs rapidly inflated and deflated to deliver. The same was true for what remained of his men.

"How do we... catch that... damned... rat!" panted one of Gelmar's men. "He... killed Gotthard!"

Gelmar clenched his jaw so hard that veins in his forehead pulsated. "If I knew, he wouldn't be alive right now, would he? Eight of you come with me and the rest stay—"

He stopped mid-sentence. *There are only eighteen of my men gathered here*, he realized. *Where are the rest?* He hesitantly looked backwards to Lev's formation behind him.

The rest of his men had been pushed back by the shield bearers and spearmen, the latter of which appeared to have doubled in number. From the new additions' lighter attire, Gelmar concluded that the slingers from before had switched their gear.

Another eight of Gelmar's men had fallen to the spearmen, who in turn, aside from one fatal injury, seemed only to have sustained minor wounds.

Gelmar's remaining men desperately tried to break through, hoping to avoid the other formation that was now closing in on them from the back, but they numbered too few now to do so.

Gelmar stood frozen as he saw his men struggle against the shield wall in the front. They were crying, cursing, and even begging to be let through before the wall pushed them back into the spears of the other formation arriving behind them. He closed his eyes as he heard the screams of his men as they thrashed for their life. He kept his eyes closed as they, with their last breaths, wailed and cursed. Cursing the fates, cursing their enemies, and cursing Gelmar for bringing them to this fate.

    "B-Boss... Are you... crying?"

CHAPTER 13
ORIGINS

"Are you alright?"

Lev's shouting voice was barely audible.

"Wh-Who are you? State your Eurasian ID!" Eric screamed, his eyes blinded and ears deafened by a flash grenade that had been thrown at him seconds ago.

"My EU-ID is 2406. Private Lev" Lev responded.

"What?" Eric yelped.

"I said my EU-ID is twenty-four-zero-six. Private Lev," Lev responded, from closer this time.

"*What?*" Eric repeated.

"I *said*, my EU-ID is— dammit, you, I'm with the Technocracy! The EU!"

Eric, squinting, could just make out Lev's general shape. As his vision slowly returned, he recognized the colours of the EU on Lev's standard-issue, private-ranked MCS model. "Alright, 2406— I mean, Lev, is there a way to contact the neutral zone's HQ? I think there's something wrong with my MCS."

Lev glanced at the display on his right wrist, swiftly opened a few sub-tabs, and took out his dog tag to confirm his ID on his local device. He waited for the device to establish a connection, only to find the connection between his squad and HQ had been broken.

"Sir, the line is dead. We can't make contact."

Eric blinked faster and harder, still trying to regain his vision. "Lev, tell me," he said, "did we lose?"

Lev surveyed the battlefield. Unidentifiable limbs and mangled cadavers could be seen far and wide. Wrecked vehicles, broken MCSs, and twisted guns created a gory scene.

Looks like I'm in hell again, Lev concluded. *When will I finally gain my freedom?*

The confused corporal desperately dug his hands in and out of his pockets, searching for his own display. "Looks like we're out of options, Lev. We might be the only ones left here— wait, what's that sound—"

"Mortar!" Lev yelled. Both of them threw themselves to the ground. The mortar shell exploded near them; debris grazed their bodies.

"Aaaarrghhh!" Eric screamed in agony. One of the fragments had passed through a small gap in his MCS near his left thigh.

Lev examined Eric's wound. *His MCS must've been damaged during the fight,* Lev concluded.

Eric tried to stand back up, but the pain was too much for him. He propped himself up on his right arm and moved his left hand shakily towards the now-exposed wound.

"Alright, Eric, listen to me," Lev began. "I've been in this situation countless times. Lie down on one side and let me patch this up." Lev took out his dog tag and tapped it on Eric's MCS to release the reserve first-aid kit from a pod on Eric's back. "Then we'll just have to locate a valid contact point in order to re-establish contact with N-Z HQ."

"And *how* are we supposed to reach that point?" Eric retorted, vision still blurred. "Are we supposed to walk straight into the enemy's fire? Can I even walk like thi— Ouch! *Watch it!*" Eric yelped. Lev had used a medical magnet to extract the fragments, poured some alcohol on the wound, and wrapped the wound with field dressing.

"There. You're good to go," Lev calmly replied with a tinge of irritation.

The scared corporal's vision was finally recovering. "God, how did we survive this massacre? We really are the sole survivors— *Eeek!*" Eric had lifted his left foot and discovered that he had been sitting on a mangled corpse all this time. He frantically made out words on the corpse's dog tag: *Mark. Sergeant.*

"Oh, God, I think I'm gonna be sick—"

"You're new to the neutral zone, aren't you? Where did you serve before this?"

"I-I served as a reserve in the fourth regiment of the fifth defence force."

"Ah, the blaue adler. So you're a rear trooper, and a reserve one at that... That's just great—"

"Don't mock me or the blaue adler! We're what's blocking the imperials in the southwest of the EU! I might not have experienced as much as you, but my friends and I have faced the imperials, too! We served as backup in the neutral zone and scored a *victory* against those pieces of shit!"

Lev smiled wryly. "Good. You do have a spine. I didn't mean anything against your previous regiment, but I just needed to give you a little push."

"A push?" Eric was incredulous.

"Do you still want to puke?"

"Um... Actually, no."

"Good. You'll have to endure the pain a little longer. We just need to escape the enemy's sight. It'll take a while to get to a valid contact point, but we'll at least make it in one piece." Lev gestured a path to safety.

Eric struggled to his feet. "Are there still enemies here? How do we find the contact point?"

"To answer your first question, I don't know how they do it in other places, but in the neutral zone, the imperials always send a final wave of men to hunt down EU survivors," replied Lev in a low voice. He pointed to the ruins of a tank nearby, subtly directing Eric to follow. "To answer your second question, the contact points are already saved in my map. Let's head out while we still can."

Eric nodded, then hobbled to the tank, following Lev. Eric grabbed the tank's surface with his left hand for balance and felt something squishy. He looked to his left and found his hand inside a breach in the tank's shell, his finger caught on what felt like a cord. When he slowly removed his hand from the hole, he heard a soft snap. His palm was covered in blood; a single eyeball dangled from his finger.

Lev heard a scream that was now familiar to him. He thought it unnecessary to turn around.

"Are you done, corporal?" he asked Eric once the screaming had abated. Lev waited patiently; he heard Eric spit.

"Yes," Eric replied. "Excuse me." He spat again, vomit still dripping down his chin.

* * *

Six Years Ago, Frankreich—Eurasian Territory

"So, Eric, you're going back to the military?"

"I guess so. Seems that's the only way to get full citizenship."

"Why? You've already been granted limited citizenship by the United Council."

Eric counted himself as one of the "lucky" victims of the levy system. He had spent four years in combat in a location that was peaceful compared to the neutral zone, but during his fifth year, he had been reassigned to the neutral zone, which, at the time, the higher-ups had deemed insufficiently supplied with Eurasian soldiers.

When Eric, following orders, had left those dreaded trenches to charge at his enemies, he had expected to be dead or grievously injured in mere seconds—and he was right. An artillery shell had exploded near him, blowing off his left arm and right leg in an instant. He had woken up days later in a field hospital behind the Eurasian frontline. Given the situation, he had been promptly sent back home, his civilian status raised to limited citizenship.

Eric cursed his circumstances. He was so close, yet so far away from full citizenship. Filled with regret and sorrow, he resigned himself to another ten years of service. With the last of the veteran money he had received after being sent home, he had bought artificial limbs from the cloning labs and upgraded his eyes with night vision via the newest innovations in biotechnology.

After losing his limbs, he had sought to become a general in the Eurasian army and to change the aged Eurasian trench doctrine to match the Imperial's modern mobile warfare doctrine.

Eric took a sip from his coffee. *You're my wife*, he thought. *You should know limited citizenship isn't an option!* The more he thought, the more frustrated he became with her.

"Eric, I need you here! We promised each other we'd live our lives to the fullest together, not die in some unknown trench! You told me that if we got limited citizenship, you would accept Macmaran's offer to work in the mines..."

Eric disregarded his wife's words. Determination in his eyes, he wordlessly opened the door and turned to face his now-enraged wife one last time.

"To do what? To work myself to death? To slave myself away to some bourgeois scientist who has connections in the United Council? I don't want to work for him or anyone supporting this wretched technocracy!"

The door slammed shut behind him.

* * *

Neutral Zone—Eurasian Frontline

"It's getting late. Let's take shelter and sleep for a bit."

Lev opened the hatch of the destroyed tank's turret. He checked for salvageable supplies, and carefully replenished his and Eric's plasma supply before making space to rest.

"A lord of humans," Eric mumbled, looking straight into Lev's eyes.

"A what?"

"Lev, if you had the power to change society, to change the Technocracy, what would you do?"

"You know, Eric, I'll know what to do once I survive this battle. Get some rest." But Lev already knew what he would do.

A while back, while watching Eric writing in a field manual, Lev had speculated that Eric was drafting a letter to his wife or an acquaintance. Letting his curiosity get the better of him, he had snuck a peek at Eric's field manual afterward. What he'd found had far surpassed his expectations from the meek rear guardsman—Eric had written at length about his hate for the technocracy, as well as how corrupt the current battle doctrine was.

For Lev, who knew that he would need every single shard of aid left in this broken world to ultimately accomplish his goal of mass reformation, it was clear. Fate had gifted him this encounter. Eric could be one of those shards.

The deadly and old trench warfare doctrine dated from the old wars before the technocracy had formed. But still, the Technocracy followed it, throwing waves of men at the enemy. In contrast, the Empire employed modern mobile warfare, which had seen great success in recent years in the neutral zone. It used a combination of tanks and other vehicles to blitz the enemy with speed and vigour. The speed of these vehicles could easily outmanoeuvre running soldiers and swiftly destroy the batteries of support artillery in the rear.

Even though Eric knew little about war and lacked experience, he knew from his fatal injuries and the efficiency of mobile warfare that trench doctrine had no place in this time and age.

Lev knew that something had to be up in the core of the Technocracy. Why would they use such an aged doctrine? Was it to clean out the slums? To throw meat at the meat grinder until there was nothing left?

Twenty-five Years Ago, Slums of Neue Berlin, Capital of Eurasia

"Schweinhund!" yelled an old baker at a child running away into one of the dark alleys of the slums.

"This kid... He always manages to steal my bread!" growled the baker with hate in his eyes. It was already hard to earn a profit in this hellhole without thieves stealing from him.

"What's worrying you so much, old man?"

"Ah, finally, the police arrived. Better late than never, am I right?" The baker said with a sneer.

The officer revealed a smirk, slightly agitated by the baker's remark. "You know how expensive bread is these days. Let the kid have some food."

After the economic collapse caused by continuous wars and setbacks to the asteroid mining project, prices had inflated drastically, causing most of the population to suffer from poor living conditions. The parliament of Neue Berlin had tried to limit the damage caused by the war by investing most of its budget into various stocks—which in turn had limited its abilities to invest into solutions to help the lower and middle class in Neue Berlin.

"What? How could you let a kid who's defying the law just do whatever he wants? Ten thousand marks' worth of bread is what he's stolen from me, officer! Ten thousand!"

The officer grasped in his pocket and revealed a wallet. "Take this as payment then. Ten thousand marks for the bread that the kid stole."

The now baffled baker looked at the officer and took the money. "If you insist, but don't blame me when I refuse to give you a refund."

"I won't."

"Leonard, how did you manage to get this bread?" Ann, one the youngest and last caretakers at the orphanage asked Leonard.

"I—"

"You stole it, didn't you?" Ann said with a sad tone.

Kinder Orphanage Neue Berlin could be read at the entrance of the building. An orphanage for the children in the slums, the lower class— the class that the United Council didn't recognize. They were subhuman scum, only ever addressed by their EU-ID. Spoiled meat, whose only purpose was to be used on the frontlines of wars so that more "qualified" individuals could relax in the back.

The entrance door opened, an officer standing in its opening.

"Miss, is this your kid?"

"Y-Yes, he is one of the kids I oversee," Ann replied nervously. "We'll return the bread if this is why you came."

The officer looked at Leonard, who was now scared, hiding behind Ann and visibly shaking from the officer's striking uniform. The uniform was emblazoned with the logo of the Eurasische Polizei (Eurasian Police). The EP were known to take out their frustrations on the lower class in the slums, charging innocent people with meaningless crimes and beating them down if they ever dared to complain.

"Don't worry, I paid for it."

This shocked Ann. Why would an EP pay for bread that one of her kids had stolen?

"Y-You p-p-paid? H-How much do we owe you?"

The officer now started laughing, reminding Leonard of the countless beatings he'd received from middle-class kids after trying to sneak from his home in the lower slum to the upper parts of Neue Berlin. They would always laugh like that after having their fun with him.

"Don't worry, the bread's on me."

He walked towards the entrance and said one last sentence before leaving.

"You know, that kid Lev could be a great officer one day."

"Why'd you say that?" Ann asked.

"He seems like the type that always manages to go against the law but yet, does something good by breaking the law."

The officer walked away, into the rain, leaving the confused but grateful Leonard and Ann behind. This encounter, although rare, didn't change Lev's hate for the Technocracy. Rather, it showed a way out, a way to start something new from nothing.

Neutral Zone—Eurasian Frontline

"Wake up, Corp. We've got visitors—explosive ones!" yelled Lev, bringing out his MCR-17.

Eric awoke with a start, disoriented by his surroundings. He wailed in fear as the rain of bullets began.

"First wave! Attack!"

"Aye-aye, sir!"

A flute could be heard coming from one of the now occupied trenches.

"What's happening, Lev?!"

"Seems like the 117th Eurasian Division's finally reached this frontline." Lev directed Eric's attention to the scores of Eurasian soldiers peeking from their trenches, watching their comrades in the first wave being slaughtered.

"Does that mean that we don't have to contact HQ?"

Lev regarded the fresh soldiers, pouring into the battlefield, dying one by one under the enemies' fire. "No, we still have to contact HQ."

"What do you mean? They're right there! They can *save* us!"

"Just wait, Corp. You'll see what I mean. I've been in these fields countless times."

A deafening blast could be heard from miles away. Lev knew this sound all too well.

"It's coming. Grab something, Corp—you'll need something to hold when it hits."

"When *what* hits?" squealed the corporal, hastily grabbing the tank's inner hatch and holding tight.

A railgun-class artillery shell headed straight towards the trenches.

"Here it comes." Lev knew that most of the soldiers would be incinerated when the blast hit the ground.

One by one the soldiers evaporated, leaving dust behind. Lev and Eric heard the soldiers who were partly incinerated screaming in pain. They could do little more than look at their mangled allies immobilized by the horror unfolding before them.

"Oh, God," Eric muttered.

Lev squeezed his eyes shut. "There are neither gods nor demons here, Eric. Only death and the dying."

THAT KID COULD BE A GREAT OFFICER ONE DAY

CHAPTER 14
SPOILS OF WAR

"Had enough?" taunted the worst voice Gelmar had ever heard in his life, from a safe distance. That voice made him feel more disgusted than that of his own whore mother, who had used to vent her frustrations on him whenever she returned home from work.

He glared—through tears, though he would never admit it—at Lev, who smugly held his hands behind his back.

"You monster! You ruined everything!"

"On the contrary. You ruined everything," replied Lev, bemused.

"What did you say!"

"I said, *you* ruined everything, for both yourself and your men," remarked Lev, beginning to pace in a circular path around the hapless Gelmar. "Wasn't it you who was overconfident? Wasn't it you who let his emotions get the better of him? Wasn't it you who kept underestimating us? Wasn't it you who killed your men by falling into every trap I set? Wasn't it you who made your men helpless by not allowing anyone to be your second in command?" Lev stopped walking. "Unlike you, I did some research on whom I was facing, and I learned that you got rid of anyone who could ever have challenged your leadership." Lev turned to face Gelmar. "Give up. You never had a chance."

"So you can kill us that easily? Like you'd allow us to live! Better take you down with us than die without a fight!" said one of the men.

Lev shrugged. "I'd honestly spare all of you—well, except for your leader, of course—because I would gain nothing from killing you. And even if you killed me, unlike your 'wise' leader, I've been training a substitute. How do you think my men were able to follow my plans to the letter?" Lev took a breath. "So what do you choose—follow your leader to the afterlife, or stay alive with me?"

"You think Vyrga would let them live just like that? He'd want to make an example!" Gelmar boomed.

Lev sighed. "I'm not certain whether he'll let them live, but they have a higher chance of survival this way, right? Did Vyrga give any indication that he's trying to justify killing anyone other than you? Besides, haven't your men done enough? Your men fought for you, bled for you, died for you. They did their best. The problem was with the task, not them, so why would Vyrga punish them? Or is it that you're just using them again to save your skin?" he accused.

"Gelmar. Let me run through a scenario, here. If your men had killed me, my men would have retaliated. Unable to withdraw with your troops, you would have sent them all to their deaths to clear out a path of escape for yourself. Having escaped, you would still be subject to Vyrga's wrath, but as you'd have completed your mission, your life would have been spared, yes?"

"Is that true, boss?"

Gelmar was almost too shocked to speak. "What! No—"

"He did say that Vyrga would slaughter us if we don't kill this guy, but maybe Vyrga would only kill him! We're just grunts!"

"Why, you dirty—"

"Would we really live?"

"Don't believ— Aaaah!" screamed Gelmar in pain as one of his men stabbed him in the back. Gelmar immediately turned around and swung his copper axe towards the man's head, killing him instantly.

He was surrounded as twelve of his remaining men pointed their weapons at him, while the other six just stood aside, not wanting to participate in this betrayal yet not planning on stopping it.

"Sorry, boss."

"It's your fault, so don't blame us."

"You wanted to be the next enlightened one, hah!"

"I have kids, boss."

"I never liked you."

Gelmar snickered, then erupted into full-on laughter.

"What's so funny?" asked the biggest one of the traitors as he brandished his axe.

"I just realized," Gelmar replied, " that none of you are worth shit." He swiftly kicked his former lackey in the stomach before snatching his axe and lodging it into the lackey's temple.

"Get him!" yelled another. He thrust his spear towards Gelmar, who dodged to the left, grabbed the incoming spear just below the spearhead, and pulled it backwards past his waist, stabbing the goon behind him. In quick succession, Gelmar bashed the spear-wielder with his shield before grabbing the handle of his axe with both hands to pull it out of the large one's head.

Just then, one of the other men swung his club towards Gelmar's head. Gelmar dodged to the right, taking the hit to his left shoulder instead. He growled in pain before swinging his newly freed axe towards the club-wielder, who managed to raise his shield in time for Gelmar to embed his axe in it. With but a single working arm, Gelmar struggled to pull his axe out of the shield, sustaining a stab to his flank and a slash to his back before he was able to swing again.

Axe back in hand, he grit his teeth and braced his core to stay on his feet. This pain and sense of despair reminded him of his past, the past he had wanted to forget but never could. As he pondered how things had come to this, he remembered something he had long forgotten: his gratitude to the one who had given him a purpose, the one he now wanted to overthrow for his own petty ambition—Vyrga. Gelmar had betrayed Vyrga for lesser reasons than the thugs had betrayed him for.

How could I do that? he asked himself as he received another stab, coughing up blood.

Impact after impact, wound after wound, his body reached its limit. He dropped his axe and tattered shield, and fell to his knees. He looked towards Vyrga's forces far in the distance, muttering "forgive me" over and over.

One of his ex-subordinates plucked his axe from the ground, hoisted it high, and ceremoniously dropped it down on its master's head.

* * *

"So how many men did we lose?" Lev asked Volker after meeting him. Even though they had just won their first major battle, Lev paced back and forth, mentally running through the next steps in his plan.

"Only... Askan and Rudolf, sir," replied Volker, suppressing his tears. He was happy that they had won with minimal losses, but they had lost two of their comrades in the battle. Even minimal losses were still losses.

"Tell five men to guard their corpses. We'll be returning them to their families." Lev continued pacing.

"Do you think their families will be able to handle the loss?"

Lev stopped pacing. "Those two were heroes. Their families might hate me, but I'll always respect them no matter what."

"You're a great man, Mr. Gher— I mean sir."

"Hah!" Lev smiled sardonically. "Remember this, Volk. Most great men are monsters."

"Don't we all have our demons? Don't be hard on yourself, sir. There must be some good in you, or why would you have spared those thugs?"

I didn't exactly spare them. I threw them to Vyrga, Lev thought to himself. Much to his dismay, a naïve part of him felt guilt and disgust at this action.

While muttering excuses to himself, Lev saw Rak and Hem approaching. Hem spoke first, before Rak could even open his mouth.

"Hey, kid! Nice slaughter! I would've called it a battle but we all know that... it... sorry, boss," apologized the large bogey with his boisterous voice turning into a whisper once he realized that Rak was glaring at him.

"Never mind," Rak replied. He turned to Lev. "Though, he was right. Nice job on winning the battle."

"Thanks, but I'm sure you're not here just to compliment me."

Rak chuckled. "Yeah, I came to remind you to give me my part of the loot. We didn't fight, but we did help you out, so this does count as a joint operation. And as we agreed, you only get a third of the loot while I keep the rest." Rak put his hand on Lev's shoulder. "But your men did all the fighting, so it wouldn't be fair to take so much. I'll just take half instead."

Rak expected Gherm to yell or cry about how unfair his proposal was, but was surprised as Lev chuckled heartily. "Isn't half too much for you? You said it yourself, *we* were the ones who fought. Let's make it eight out of ten for me."

Rak's eyes narrowed, but he kept his smile. "So you want to haggle, huh?" Haggling was an important aspect of bogey culture: the vast majority of bogeys were good with numbers and trading, so almost all bogeys haggled, both with gods and with each other in everyday life. After the subjugation of the greyborn bloodline, it was only natural that the upper classes would implement the merit system to incentivise slaves without paying them actual money.

Rak pointed at a few of the retrieved lead bullets and caltrops. "You did fight by yourself and win with minimal losses, but it wouldn't have been possible if I hadn't helped you negotiate with the other hidden smiths in my territory. I insist on splitting the spoils in half."

"You wouldn't have gotten anything and Gelmar would still be alive if my army had failed. Not only did we get rid of one of your enemy's leaders, but you also gained some loot without losing any men. Seven to three."

"He was a mere annoyance. Furthermore, I helped you in finding the families of his victims. Four to six."

"Yes you did, but I was the one who convinced them to come. Still seven to three,, but you also get to keep the copper axe."

Rak thought about the offer and shrugged "Deal."

"Glad we could come to an agreement. Now if you'll excuse me, we have to start looting before those damned black lizards try to steal them and ruin their clothes."

"Damned corpse-eaters," Rak growled. "Fine. We also have to go." He turned to his companion. "Hem."

"Sure thing, boss. Bye, kid." said Hem before following Rak. Volker at his side, Lev watched Rak and Hem leave.

"I really don't like that guy, sir," said Volker.

"We don't have to like him, Volk. We just have to get along until one side either stops benefitting the other or joins them."

"I don't think I'll be joining under anyone similar to that brute anytime soon, sir."

"Why? Did something happen between you two?"

"Well, boss. Let's just say I ended up with a broken arm and my family ended up with less pots to sell, about five less pots to sell. That overgrown asshole's too dumb to apologize to someone once he bumps into them." growled the young lad.

Lev blinked in surprise before breaking out in laughter, confusing Volker.

"Hahaha! Sorry, I didn't think you could even be that daring. Now, come along. We have a busy ten days ahead of us."

"Sure thing, sir."

CHAPTER 15

SLANDER AND BANTER

Ten days had passed since the slaughter, and though at the time the result of the events had been on everyone's tongue, news finally quieted down as time for an even more important one arrived. It was time for the expedition.

Throughout the cavern, more than three hundred bogeys were to gather right outside the wall separating their territory from that of the cavern's monsters. Guards and warriors had cleared the area on both sides of the wall of hostiles in order to keep the mining slaves safe and productive, but as always, the expedition was slated to proceed far beyond the safe zone.

Plodding towards the gathering from the slave quarters were Lev and Volker, who had met up on the way to the rendezvous point. Each carried a shield, a spear, and a cross-shaped pole with a sack tied to it. Inside the sacks were waterskins, food, spare clothes, food preparation tools, clay serving and eating utensils, and others.

The streets were uncharacteristically quiet, aside from the pitter-patter of their footsteps, the soft sloshing of their waterskins, and the occasional sound leakage from the nearby houses. Aside from most of the chosen adults and youths, who had already arrived at the rendezvous point, no one was out—those not chosen for the expedition had holed themselves up inside their homes. The goblins tended to be *rowdy* when they arrived.

Lev and Volker had just reached the dilapidated south-western quarters. It seemed that because neither of them had participated in the expedition two years prior, both of them had been chosen to participate in this year's.

Volker was unaccustomed to the continued silence. Usually, by this point, Lev would have briefed him on their future plans, discussed strategies, or asked for advice if the need arose. When Lev was this silent, it could only mean one thing.

"Um... Sir?"

"What?" Lev was trying to stand on his tiptoes to size up the crowd.

"I don't mean to be rude, but is something bothering you today? You look... troubled."

"I'm not troubled," replied Lev calmly, craning his neck.

"You're too calm right now, sir. From my observations, you're usually calm, but when you're *too* calm, it means you're angry about something," explained Volker.

Lev blinked, then turned to face Volker. "What else have you noticed?" he asked, his curiosity piqued. In his past life, before entering the world of politics, he had continuously practiced modulating his body language and facial expressions to prevent others from reading him like a book. It seemed that, for this second life, he needed to master his old skills anew.

"Um... You love to smile? Don't look at me like that, sir. You really do. You smile all the time and the only time you don't smile is when something inconveniences you, pisses you off, or makes you want to kill it."

"Is that so?"

"Yes, sir, it is so."

"I see," Lev replied as he contemplated what he had just heard. He needed to pay more attention to his actions until he had better control over himself. "Anything else?"

"Nothing else to report, sir," replied Volker before continuing his previous inquiry. "Would you please tell me what happened before we met?"

Lev broke eye contact and consciously cleared his face of any tells. "Let's just say it was something annoying."

"Ah, your sister," blurted out Volker thoughtlessly.

Lev's seething stare shone its white-hot spotlight upon the defenseless Volker again. "Apologies, sir! I didn't mean it like that!" he said in a panic.

As though by magic, Lev's face returned to neutral. "Just think before you speak next time. For future reference, you're not wrong. She kept shrieking about how I shouldn't have done what I did, and how there was no way to avoid a war with Vyrga."

"With all due respect, that's her personality, sir. As your sister, she's been supporting the both of you, and she does have your best interest at heart. You've been spending your merits on equipment for us, right? It must be hard for her. Everything's getting more expensive. Speaking of, why *is* everything getting more expensive?"

"Haven't you noticed? According to our informants, fewer supplies are coming from the outside. Many greyborns are stocking up on long-lasting food like grains. Because of the increased demand, many others now can no longer afford to buy food for their families. If they weren't willing to settle for cave moss, they'd all be dead."

"Oh, gods," Volker whispered. "You don't think—"

"There's a shortage? I believe so." Lev replied, though he feared it was worse than a mere shortage of supplies. He feared that the situation could evolve into a famine.

Volker shuddered. "Let's return to our previous topic, sir. As I was saying, your sister has your best interests at heart, though she can be—"

Lev held his hand up to cut Volker off. "Overly dramatic?"

"Yes, that's the word. But is there anything else that's bothering you?

You grew up with her antics. They can't be the only thing."

Lev rubbed his forehead uncharacteristically. "I was berated by the lover boy."

"Lover boy?"

"Thorst."

"That easy-going guard who looks like he'd keep smiling through an earthquake?"

"Yup."

Volker's eyes widened. "He likes her? Why would he?" he blurted out before covering his mouth.

"Volker. You would do well to remember that she's my *sister*."

"Sorry, Mr. Gher— sir."

Lev grinned. "Apology accepted. You really should watch what you say, though. I'm glad that you're opening up to me, but there are times where you should think before you speak."

"Sorry..."

Lev smiled gently as he saw the kid lower his head. "No worries. Anyway, back to the previous discussion. Yes, he does care about her and despite his act of trying to be nonchalant and uncaring, he can get quite... emotional whenever he believes my actions would endanger her."

"Really? I heard he didn't seem that different when you talked after the knife fight with the thugs."

"Everyone has a limit, Volk. And the closer you get to it, the more irrational and troublesome people act."

"What did he say?"

Lev frowned before answering. "That I'm a danger to her life and how I turned out to be an ungrateful scumbag like the rest of the ambitious thugs which give greyborns a bad name. The worst part is when he said how better off she would be if I didn't exist since I only leech off of her and give nothing in return."

"He said that? The only guard who lets us off if he finds us taking unauthorized breaks?"guy

"He was emotional at the moment, as I did kill one of Vyrga's elites. What do you think would happen if, in the future, I lose to Vyrga? What do you think he would do to her? Thorst would try to protect her, of course, but how long would he be able to do that?"

"I can understand where he's coming from."

"Me too, but the last thing I needed was him shouting in my ears moments after she did. My head can only withstand so many headaches."

"I feel sorry for you, sir."

"I'd feel sorry for myself too, if I were in your shoes. Well, it seems we're almost there," Lev said with a smile as they approached the gates. They were crowded with bogeys of all colours from greyborn slaves to bluish-green nobles, though there were separate lines to separate the bogeys by status and reduce the chance of any conflicts between them.

No matter a goblinoid's status, everyone had to wait in line, and once it was finally their turn, they were stopped by an old pale green bogey.

"Hey, kid. I heard you were busy," he said in a disappointed tone.

"I did what needed to be done, Kul," Lev replied with a blank expression.

"But was it the right thing to do? At first, I didn't mind that you made your own crew, but don't you think you took it too far?"

"Before I answer your questions, let me ask one of my own. Is protecting oneself a crime?"

"Yourself? No, it's not. But making others kill for your ambition? Definitely one in my book. I've seen nobles, Gherm, and lately, you've been acting like one. Why allow innocents to kill and die for you? Wasn't the reason that you formed a group to protect the oppressed from thugs, not to become like them? Why allow your men to bloody their hands instead of telling the guards?"

"We did tell the guards, Mr. Kul," Volker interrupted, grabbing Kul's attention.

"You did? Why didn't anybody tell me about it?" asked Kul dumbfounded.

Lev coughed, shifting Kul's attention back to himself. "You know there are factions among the guards and warriors. Even if you did find out, the others wouldn't have let you interfere even if they had to stop you with force. And let's say you managed to stop Gelmar. By relying on you, we'd be saying to Rak, Vyrga, and everyone else that we're too weak to fend for ourselves.

"If we didn't stop them ourselves, they'd trample us once you or the other guards on your side happen to be looking into other matters. As horrible as it was to waste so many lives, it was a necessity to protect ourselves and our loved ones. Or tell me Kul, can you say otherwise?" ended Lev while staring straight into Kul's eyes turning it into a contest of wills.

In the end, Kul looked away. "Fine! You're right! It was the only way!"

Lev smiled. "Good thing that we agree on that part. Now if you'll excuse us, we, unfortunately, were conscripted to be part of the expedition. We have to get there before we're accused of desertion."

Kul sighed and moved aside allowing the two to continue on their way.

"Thank you. Now come along, Volk. We're already late as it is."

Just as they were about to pass through the gates, Kul yelled, "Wait!"

"Oh, come on! Get on with it!" yelled a bystander who had been waiting behind Lev and Volker, who promptly shut up after a single glare from Kul. "Sorry... "

"Alright. What is it?" Lev replied, a little bothered at being stopped again.

"Just one last question. Do you think Gat, if he were still here with us, would accept what you're becoming?" said Kul in a sorrowful tone.

"Father..." muttered Lev as he felt a twinge of pain in his heart as the image of the one who was his father, yet was not his father, flashed in his mind. Another part of him missed Gat a great deal.

"I don't know what you'll do in the future, but please don't disappoint him by becoming one of those monsters."

Lev managed to compose himself and said with a determined look, "Though I won't yield to them, I won't become like them. I can promise you that my plans involve making life better, not only for me and my men, but also for all those I can save from their tyrants. There will be change and I can assure it will be for the better."

"How?" asked Kul.

Lev grinned. "Just wait and see. For now, we have an expedition to go to, but once we're back, there will be a world of change."

Just as he finished his sentence, Lev turned around and left with Volker by his side.

"What a show-off, am I right?" said the earlier bystander, nudging the stunned Kul on the shoulder. That confident grin had reminded Kul of Gherm's father.

Kul glared at the bogey. "Do I look like I'm your friend? Touch me again and you're going to the back of the line!" he growled.

"Sorry," the bystander mumbled once again.

Good luck, kid, you'll need it, thought Kul with a sigh before resuming his duty once more.

CHAPTER 16
EYE FOR AN EYE

Lev and Volker had finally reached the expedition site. Shouts, curses and laughter filled the place as crowds of bogeys from different walks of life awaited the arrival of their goblin overlords. Some were excited for the chance to keep some of the lower quality materials and artefacts found in the lower levels; others were dismayed at being forced to join what would likely be a death march.

While Lev kept a stoic expression as he searched for his men and kept an eye out for danger, Volker was baffled by the sights he was seeing. It was his first time seeing so many commoners and nobles beyond the wall. His parents had always kept him away from seeing the previous expeditions, even when it had come time for his brother to join one two years ago. They had feared that he would be targeted by the fouler members of society and be manipulated by them since, despite his intelligence, he was quite naïve. They were already furious that he had decided to join Lev's band—if he had not been forced to join the expedition this year, they would not have allowed him to be here.

He kept looking at the mishmash of outfits, ranging from the white tunics and shirts of the commoners, to the fancy attires of the richer nobles decorated with slightly uncommon jewels and fine metals.

Lev, on the other hand, found them unimpressive. To his eyes, though the quality of their hemp and leather clothes wasn't bad, it wasn't something that would impress him. He also felt that behind this facade of joy and excitement displayed by the more boisterous of the conscripts, there was a tense air filled with fear and worry. In the end, even dreamers and fortune seekers were just like everybody else—afraid to die.

Instead of gawking at a bunch of strangers, Lev thought it would be a better use of their time if Volker helped in locating both Lev and Rak's men. Both groups decided to join together early on to deter other gangs. Most were not stupid enough to do anything right before the expedition starts as it would make a convenient excuse for the goblins to toy with them, but the world was not wanting for fools.

"You really should pay better attention to your surroundings, Volk," Lev advised Volker as they kept walking with Lev making them walk near the leftmost wall.

"Um, why is that, sir? It's not like Vyrga or any of the other gang leaders are gonna harm us."

"Oh, really? Tell that to the people stalking us."

"W-We're being tailed?" asked Volker hesitantly.

"Yes. We're being tailed. Don't look back. Things might take a turn to the worse once they realize that they've been found out. Considering that they haven't done anything so far, I'm sure that they're waiting for something or someone. I believe that there are more ahead and they're trying to either block our way or surround us. It'll be better to—"

Lev stopped talking as he suddenly felt murderous intent from his right. He immediately ducked, avoiding an arrow before turning and locking eyes with its owner. In the end, he found a greyborn that he thought shouldn't be here as he looked younger than Volker, glaring at him and trying to knock another stone-headed arrow to his self-bow.

Guess this is whom they had been waiting for. Must be Heimo, Lev thought as the boy's image corresponded with what he had in mind. He was one of Vyrga's youngest disciples and was really close to the late Gelmar. He was also one of the few greyborns who knew how to use a bow, and due to his talents and contributions, was one of two primary candidates to succeed Vyrga in the future. It was known that though he seemed the kindest of Vyrga's elites, all it took was one order from Vyrga for him to slaughter not only his target but also his entire family.

After Vyrga took over the man's territory, Heimo killed everyone including the women and children, even though Vyrga had only requested that the man and his eldest sons be killed. When Vyrga asked him why he did that, Heimo just shrugged and replied that despite it being distasteful it was a necessity as even if the children didn't want revenge once they grew up, the mother, grandmother, grandfather, uncles, aunts, cousins, nieces might bring harm to them in the future if fate allows it, it was better to be a merciless pragmatist than a merciful fool.

Lev was about to tell Volker to get ready, only to see him throw his marching pack on the ground and take a combat stance with both his shield and spear raised. This caused Lev to smile. "Looks like he's learning."

"Are you alright, sir?" asked the young lad nervously.

"For now, calm yourself. It's time for battle."

Volker nodded, his expression turning wary and guarded. "I'm ready."

Suddenly a robed man pushed his way through the nearby crowd and charged at Lev, knife in hand, only to have his face slammed by Lev's marching pack. As the figure staggered backwards, he felt a sharp pain in his abdomen as it was penetrated by Lev's spear.

The crowd screamed in shock and terror as they saw Lev slam the stunned thug with his shield while pulling his spear from the robed man's guts causing his entrails, which were entangled on the spear, to spill on the ground. The crowd then moved aside to give a wide berth to the combatants, not wanting to get harmed in the process.

"Back off!" yelled Volker as another robed bogey staggered backwards. Lev saw the robed bogey grit his teeth as he retreated, bleeding from a wound on his thigh.

"Arrow!" Lev yelled. Volker glanced over, and raised his shield just in time to block an incoming arrow.

Lev immediately spotted another bogey pushing his way through a group of three while approaching him from the left side. Lev immediately glared at him and pointed his spear at the figure. "Don't even dare."

The figure backed away into the crowd, waiting for more of his companions to gather before committing to an attack.

Volker pointed his spear at the attackers, ready to take the life of any assailants. "Sir! How many are there?"

"Who knows—"

Lev was interrupted as an arrow slammed into his shield.

"Who knows? Just don't let your guard down. Even if you hear some of our guys shouting, don't let your guard down!"

Two more robed figures approached from his front. They tried charging Lev at the same time, only for one to be immediately speared through the head. The other was shoved back by Lev's shield, and when he tried to dodge around it, he screamed as he was stabbed in the eye with the obsidian knife that Lev kept as a sidearm.

Another four approached, causing the crowd to move even further away—it was not their fight, and none of the guards were trying to stop it. This was definitely no mere street fight.

It was getting harder for Lev and Volker to push their enemies back, and Lev could see a look of satisfaction on Heimo's face. A look that disappeared when Lev took out a horn and blew it, startling the robed men and the nearby crowd.

More horns were blown throughout the vicinity and Lev's men rushed into the area, causing the robed men to hesitate as they contemplated between either finishing the job or running away. This was their best chance to kill Gherm, but they also needed to retreat to avoid causing a bigger scene. If they didn't fall back in time, they risked not only attracting the goblins' attention, but dying to Gherm's men.

In the end, the assassins decided to slip away. They weren't Heimo's own men, only paid professionals, and Heimo hadn't quite promised them enough money to go through all this trouble. It would be better to quit on this task and find a better target—there was ample demand for hitman services.

"So much for avoiding attention," Lev grumbled as he saw the would-be-assassins mix in with the crowd. When he turned his gaze back to Heimo's location, he saw that Heimo had also left the area.

"Are you okay, sir?" asked one of Lev's ten men as he muscled through the crowd.

"If you'd arrived a moment later, I wouldn't have been! Where were you? I believe I asked you to keep watch over the entire vicinity!" Lev told the man with a deep frown plastered on his face.

"Sorry, sir, but we were baited by Vyrga. A few moments ago it looked like that there was going to be a fight between Rak and Vyrga. As you know Vyrga has about three times the number of men, so we interfered to even the odds—"

"Leaving you unable to cover the whole area, allowing Heimo to set his trap. Is that right?"

"Yes. Thankfully, Captain Jem decided to leave some of us nearby in case you came," the man replied.

"Jem, huh..." Lev thought back to the cautious middle-aged man he assigned as a captain. Back when he had introduced the three-man formation, he had chosen a captain for each formation. Among the captains, Jem was the oldest and the most experienced in combat, as he was once the second in command for a gang ruled by a bogey named Dagga. Dagga had been known to be many things—daring, ambitious, wise, just, and loyal. He had been popular among his men, as he had kept everything fair and never targeted those who didn't deserve it. Alas, as with all good, ambitious men, he had been betrayed and killed by the greediest of his followers.

After Dagga's death, his men had fulfilled their last assignment by hunting down the traitors. But after that, the group had slowly fallen apart, until they had all separated ways.

After the collapse, Jem had continuously switched allegiances, notably serving Rak at one point, but had always left. He hadn't found in any of the leaders the qualities he was looking for. He'd eventually given up his search and chosen to live as a regular miner, until recently. It seemed that Gherm had reminded him a lot of Dagga, so he'd chosen to get his hopes up for the last time and joined the band. For the time being, he not only showed great skill and discipline, but also showed strategic prowess. He'd also been one of Lev's advisors when planning the battle against Gelmar.

Looks like I found my third-in-command, Lev mused before focusing on the waiting soldier.

"Can you forgive us, sir?" asked the soldier nervously, breaking Lev out of his thoughts.

"That will depend on how you handle this task. Gather the others, take six of them with you to check the parameter for any more surprises! And make sure not to fall to any ploys this time!" Lev ordered.

"Sir, yes, sir!" the man replied before heading off to fulfil the task.

Lev looked at the crowd and yelled, "Alright folks, the show is over! Better get ready before the goblins arrive!"

This caused the gawkers to continue on their way, as Lev was right. There were more important things to do.

"Now that they're gone, why can I ask a question, sir?" asked Volker.

"Does anyone ask an answer?" Lev replied.

"'Ask an answer'?"

"It's a joke. Everyone asks for a question or for an answer, but nobody asks an answer itself in the form of a question."

"I honestly don't get what you mean, sir."

Lev stared at his feet and sighed. "Never mind. Now, what did you want to ask?"

"Why didn't you blow the horn earlier?"

"I'd thought our men would arrive earlier so I'd wanted to keep it a secret. Yes, if they'd investigated properly they would've learned from the men we released that we use horns to commence ambushes. But, they wouldn't have known that I've supplied most of our men with horns, and we can use them to send signals and messages. If they'd tried to hunt us down on scouting missions, we'd know when a group was attacked and be able t o commence a counter-attack immediately. Now they might think up some countermeasures."

Volker shrugged. "The only countermeasure I can think of is if they find out which men have them and take them out first. But how in the world would they do that? That would require them to take out multiple men at the same time and we all know Vyrga's men aren't that good. The only thing they can do is set traps and ambush us, but how would they accomplish that on such short notice?"

"We'll see. It's better to be cautious. And a word to the wise—never underestimate your foes."

"True. We'll think of it on the way, sir, but don't you think we should go meet with the others? It's better to join them early and think of a way to deal with Vyrga," Volker asked Lev.

Lev nodded. "Let's go then. We also need more info from Rak about the other gangs joining this expedition."

And so they joined with their remaining soldiers and continued towards the gathering spot. In the end, the other six soldiers joined them once they finished searching the area and they managed to reach the rendezvous point safely.

CHAPTER 17

HAZE O' PLENTY

"*Skraaaaaaaaa!*" screeched a hiveling. Its broken body lay convulsing on the ground; its bluish-green haemolymph dripped from where its abdominal segment once was.

Lev and two of his men simultaneously pierced their spears into its head, and the yellowish light in its eyes dimmed.

It's dead... those hellish creatures... every last one of them is dead, Lev raggedly breathed.

The hiveling had managed to take down five other bogeys, one of them belonging to his group. Lev offered a silent prayer to his late ally.

Two months have passed since the expedition began, and six of his men had died before the expedition had even reached the fourth layer.

He thought back on how it had all begun. The number of men, whether goblin or bogey, was double the usual. Though past expedition teams had been composed only of only goblins and bogeys, additional reinforcements had been added to the present expedition. Along with the gaunt forms of the demoralized goblins and the appearance of new goblinoid slaves, something drastic must have happened on the surface.

Few bogeys had ever encountered other goblinoid races in the cavern, so few that the bogey consensus was that the goblins prevented contact between the enslaved races out of fear of collusion and mass uprising. Accordingly, this was the first time many commoners and greyborns encountered these different yet similar creatures.

The goblins had brought with them many goblinoids, from the ten giant yellow ones, known as bugbears, to the twenty red and muscular goblinoids with a curved horn, called dekas, that resembled a few of the horned noble-born goblins—only more vicious looking. There were also fifteen burga, a species that appeared similar to normal goblins but slightly larger, with a tail and a larger and stronger jaw; and ten dargs, a dainty, purple-skinned species of goblinoids sporting long hair and long ears that, Lev thought, looked quite similar to humans.

What was more shocking than the addition of these new peoples was that the youngest heir of the chief of the Jiira, Bulgu, was the spearhead of the expedition. First the food shortages, then doubling the number of men, the addition of newcomers, and now this? Lev was more than sure that something was wrong.

To start, the expedition force had marched after a speech from Bulgu and a recital by the shamans of the hymn of bravery. There was a tale known among goblin-kind that when Jom, the father of all, had been slain by "the one from the void," plunging the world in darkness and madness, a drop of his blood had formed a young girl with long white hair, pointy ears, and red eyes known as Zeja. Unlike the children and wife of Jom, she'd braved the dark depths of the underworld to gather the fragments of his soul and bargained with the death god Nom so that he would re-forge the fragments into one whole and revive Jom.

After reviving Jom, Zeja had gained his blessing and the right to lead the gods in the battle against "the one from the void" and his minions. She had then pushed her enemies back into the abyss of space, ending the chaos and gaining her the title of the goddess of war.

* * *

In the beginning, excluding the foreign goblinoids, the gathered expedition force had consisted of six hundred bogeys, four hundred and fifty of whom were greyborns, and a hundred and fifty goblin fighters, plus Bulgu and ten goblin nobles.

As the expedition had progressed deeper into the cave, the goblin-led army had fought against increasingly large hiveling hordes and increasingly hostile terrain for survival and resources. After clearing the first few layers, about five hundred bogeys still remained, three hundred and sixty of whom were greyborns.

"Shall we begin harvesting, sir?" someone asked Lev, causing him to break from his stupor. He turns towards the voice to find that it was Jem.

"Yes. You can begin. But do be careful."

Jem smiled. "This isn't my first expedition, sir. I'm sure everyone can now harvest the crystals from these damn things whilst they're asleep." Then, as he looked at his surroundings, his smile faded. "I wish we knew how to kill them easily in their sleep, too."

Lev could not agree more. This had been the biggest hiveling attack to date, with their numbers reaching sixteen drones. "Thankfully there weren't any warriors." He shuddered as he thought of the gigantic monstrosity that they had fought three days ago.

As they turned a corner, a gigantic hiveling, three times bigger than the one they had just slain, appeared, accompanied by three drones and a spitter. The large hiveling had larger and sharper mandibles capable of cutting a bogey in half. Its chitin was so hard that most weapons could not harm it, requiring the majority of the expedition forces to aim at its eyes and the gaps between its three body segments. Its six feet were equipped with claws so sharp that they could slash through shields, rendering them useless.

The spitter, on the other hand, was slightly smaller and physically weaker than a regular drone, but it was capable of shooting a potent acid from its abdomen that could melt the flesh of its victims. Warriors and spitters rarely appeared before the sixth layer, but as though fate were spiting them, both had attacked in tandem, killing thirty-four bogeys, five dekas, three burgas, four goblins, and a bugbear.

Lev looked at the surroundings to find an additional thirty bogeys dead with another eight more critically injured. He lamented that most, if not all of the injured, would pass away in the next few days if not treated properly. The medical supplies that they were supplied with were insufficient and the medical techniques of the witch doctors, shamans, and healers were underdeveloped.

Skilled magic could mend their wounds, but alas, frontline cannon fodder were unworthy of such life-saving techniques. Capable healers needed to be ready and available to take care of expedition leaders and nobles for the slightest graze. If one of Lev's own men were injured, he would receive first aid from Lev at best.

"Heh, looks like the kid's getting the hang of it too," said Jem as Volker poked a hole with a long-handled adze in the abdomen of a drone. The drone's digestive acid spilled onto the ground, fizzing and melting through the stone.

Along with the acid were a few yellow stones and metal balls, which were the biggest reasons for the expedition's deep progress. Hivelings were capable of refining ores, which they mixed into their wax to build their hives. And of course, these ores were extremely profitable.

Hivelings were also capable of refining haze crystals, special mana crystals that were great alchemical reagents capable of storing immense amounts of magical energy. Before refinement, though, they were corrosive to beings with low magical resistance. This was actually why greyborns had been forced to live in the caves. With their affinity for magic and native magic resistance, bogeys, especially of the greyborn variety, were the perfect candidates to mine and refine haze crystals.

In the past, when nobody had known that the hivelings were capable of curing ores and haze crystals, the expeditions had been far shorter and safer, as it had been protocol to avoid the local creatures, who in most cases, also avoided them.

However, once the goblins had discovered that hivelings were capable of neutralizing the haze crystals' corrosiveness, it had suddenly

become necessary to hunt them for what came to be known as
"refinement sacs."

Due to the greed of the goblins and their overhunting of the
hivelings, the hivelings now considered all goblinoids a threat to be
exterminated.

"Come on, you lazy louts! Harvest all the loot! You know it's worth
more than your miserable lives!" roared a vile voice.

"Gods, I hate that guy," said a certain large greyborn accompanied by
another one slightly shorter than him.

"Rak and Hem, how're the losses on your end?"

"Ten loyal men, kid. Ten loyal men," muttered Hem.

"It's all those damn goblins' fault," grunted Rak, grinding his teeth
in anger. "What are they even after? It's clear from the way they
handled the expedition and previous events that this isn't just about
some damn rocks and mere trinkets! Why are they in such a rush to kill
us all!" he roared.

"Maybe he can explain," said Lev as he pointed at another
approaching duo of greyborns.

"Vyrga and one of his pets. And it had to be Oswald." Hem spat on
the ground. He then turned to Lev. "As much as I respect you, kid, do
we really need to work with such scum?"

Everyone had realized it during the first month, but this expedition
was the wrong time and place for them to undermine each other. The
expedition had always been an opportunity for bogeys to settle
grievances with each other, as goblins had always displayed a lack of
interest in the discipline or quarrels between conscripted slaves. But this
time, things were clearly different. The decapitated head of Veer, a
leader of a small gang who had tried to kill his rival, Guru, proved that,
at least this time around, such acts were not tolerated.

Instead of just trying to avoid each other, Lev had thought it best to propose a truce, lasting at least until the end of the expedition, to Vyrga. Neither Lev or Rak were fool enough to believe that under normal circumstances, Vyrga and his men would abide by this agreement, but with the death of two gang leaders and a noble, none of them wanted to risk Bulgu's wrath. The way Lev had explained it to Rak, both of them could also use this opportunity to closely study Vyrga and his inner circle, though Vyrga would have the opportunity to study them in turn.

It was Rak who replied, "As much as I hate to say it, at the moment we do..."

"Fuck!" Hem cursed.

"It seems you're happy to see us," mocked Vyrga.

"Yeah, I'm so happy I could kill you from joy," growled Hem.

"This isn't the time for this, Hem. Not now, anyway," said Rak, wielding his axe.

Vyrga sighed. "Seems like you're still mad about my test, Rak."

"Test? *Test?* You turned my best friend against me! I *killed* him because of you! I ought to—"

"Ought to what? Kill me?" Vyrga cut in. "He was going to betray you sooner or later. If I hadn't given him the opportunity, someone else would have. Deep down, you know it was inevitable."

"Graaah!" Rak roared as he was about to bring his axe down on the calm and collected Vyrga, only to be stopped by both Lev and Hem.

"Stop, you fool! Do you want to die?" yelled Hem. "Calm down! This is an easy way for him to get rid of you without dirtying his hands!"

"Now you're calling me a fool? You think you can order me around!"

"I can't order you around, Rak, but one's actions determine their identity. Do you want everything you built to end because you fell for his ploy? For just another one of his tests?" replied Lev. "Look at your men and tell me."

Rak then realized that his men had gathered around them, and some of them were being beaten by the goblins as they tried to persuade them not to get involved. Rak calmed his wrath and took a deep breath. "I'm fine now. Let me go."

After a brief moment, Lev and Hem released him and he started walking towards his men.

"Where do you think you're going, boss?" asked Hem.

"Going to fix what we started, of course. Lev will handle everything here."

"'Lev'?" asked Oswald, who had been silent up to that point.

"That's what the kid goes by these days. You better remember it. And Hem, take care of the kid," Rak said, before going to diffuse the situation.

"Of course."

Lev turned to Vyrga. "Now, I don't believe you came here just to piss us off and try to get us killed. Mind telling us your true motive?"

Vyrga sneered. "I just was informed by a few of my acquaintances of the two main reasons for the expedition."

"And they are?"

"A mythical weapon once wielded by Ainshart, and a war between siblings to inherit the chiefdom."

CHAPTER 18
MERCENARIES AND BOUNTIES

Another three days passed safely with no further attacks from either hivelings or other local beasts, and the expedition force finally reached the fifth layer, or fifth floor, as some liked to call it. All the layers after the average-looking first one were enigmas, but the weirdest were the fifth, sixth, and seventh. The fifth layer was mostly a field of bluish-green glowing grass with spots of white glowing moss covering the ceiling, resembling what the older bogeys called stars. After the untameable forest of the sixth layer and the mind-bendingly bizarre terrain on the seventh layer, the fifth layer was the most fascinating layer currently known to both bogeys and the rest of goblinkind.

Upon arrival at these underground grasslands, Bulgu formed seven groups consisting of bogeys, burgas, and dekas and ordered them to scout ahead for valuable resources such as useful metals, unearthed artefacts, magical herbs, water sources, edible plants, and large herds of prey, and to help the expeditionary force to locate and avoid nasty surprises such as traps, ambushes, and hostile fauna.

Among these groups, one was composed of four of Lev's men, two dekas, and a single burga. That squad was just heading back to the rendezvous point to meet with the rest of the scouting groups.

"So when are you gonna tell us what the boss was mad about, captain?" inquired Gul, a known chatterbox among Lev's men and the fourth-youngest after Volker.

Volker pursed his lips. This was the thirtieth time Gul had asked today. "As always I'll give you the same answer. He wasn't mad about anything, and even if he was, how would I know? I was harvesting haze crystals. Jem was the one tailing him then."

"Come on, Volker. You're his favourite—you have to know something. The guys and I are just worried about him, you know. Can't you tell us what happened? Maybe we could help."

"You? Worried about Lev? Do you expect me to believe that?"

Gul stayed silent under Volker's scrutiny. "Alright," he sighed, "I'm just curious and a little worried that he'll piss off the wrong goblins and drag all of us into a fight he alone starts."

"Funny that that's what you're worried about, since from what we've seen, he ends fights," interrupted Molg, one of the taller and more silent followers of Lev. "I was talking to Volker, and 'Gherm' goes by Lev now. Which is another thing I wanna know. Volker, why did he change his name?"

"I honestly don't know."

"So you don't know why he was mad, and you don't know why he changed his name. Did he tell you anything?"

"He did, but it's mostly classified information."

Gul smiled mischievously. "So he's hiding his secrets from you, huh? I'm sure Jem knows. Looks like the boss prefers gruff old man Jem over young boys like you. Never thought he swung that wa— *ouch!*" he yelped as Volker bonked his helmet with the blunt end of his spear.

"Shut up, Gul. The last thing we need is you spreading another rumour."

"Well, it's not a rumour if it's true. That purple girl Varra has a thing for you. Can't blame her since you saved her from getting squished by that giant hiveling," Gul said with a grin.

"I know, but it's not the time for love and I doubt that the goblins would allow a relationship between us."

"They won't, but it's more about you being too shy to return her feelings. You keep blushing whenever she talks to you."

"I-I'm not that good with girls."

"You aren't that good with men either. It hasn't been long since we joined Lev, but little Volk's already growing up. Good thing I convinced you to join," Gul said while snickering.

Volker smiled. "Thanks for that, by the way." He still could not believe that not only had he joined a gang, something that his overprotective parents still could not accept, but he had become a part of his leader's close counsel. He had never believed that there was anything special about him, other than being perhaps marginally smarter than the other bogeys, and he had expected to end up making pottery for a living like his father did. Even though he found no joy in it, it was a fair, honest way to make a living.

Now though, with Gul's help, he had found something more to his liking. He disliked spilling the blood of others, but he enjoyed the excitement, the sense of unity, and the dream for a better future.

"What are friends for? We grew up together, Volk."

"Yup. But really though, we need to pay attention to our surroundings. Wouldn't want to be ambushed, now, would we?" Volker asked as he took a look at his surroundings to see if there was any sign of movement in the endless field of grass.

"You shouldn't worry about that. Our burga friend Rogga here has some seriously sharp senses. Heck, he can catch the scent of those insects before any of us even see them," replied the elder of the two dekas in Gul's stead. Rogga nodded in agreement before turning his attention back to their surroundings.

"That's good to hear, but we still need to pay attention in case they can hide their scent, muffle the sounds of their steps, or lie in wait underground. And sorry if we were bothering you, mister, um..."

"The name's Gozzag, kid. And there's nothing wrong with being able to have a good long conversation. Something that bugbears and goblins don't seem to get... Isn't that right, Ban?" he asked his companion, who sported a nasty scar under his left eye.

"He's right," replied the companion. "Try talking to one of them and the first thing he'll do is either growl or start a fight. I was just asking one of those green bastards for a drink, only to find him picking his knife and trying to start a fight with me." Ban sighed.

"Is that how you got that scar?" asked Gul.

"What? No. Got it from a battle with a tribe of a short-ears down south. It was fun while it lasted, but the druids had to interfere and ruin our fun."

"Short-ears? Druids?"

Ban was confused for a second about how a native of these lands was unfamiliar with druids and short-ears, but he realized soon after. "Oh, yeah... Your tribe isn't allowed to leave this place. Sorry..."

"It's not a problem."

Ban frowned. "'Not a problem,' you say? It's definitely a problem! How can you even stand to live under dirt for so long? I could never accept a life without the warmth of the sun and the beauty of the star-filled night."

Volker shrugged. "I was born into this life, so I've only seen carvings and paintings of those things. And it's not like we bogeys have never tried to reclaim our place outside. There have been many uprisings, but they were all brutally crushed by the goblins. If you want to know how horrifying the last 'war of freedom' was, there's an old green taskmaster called Kul. You can ask him once we get back."

Ban raised his left eyebrow. "Once we get back? Don't you mean if?"

"I have no intention of dying," Volker replied solemnly.

Ban smiled. "So you do have guts. Don't you have any intention of ever being free?"

"Of course I do, but I'm biding my time. Nothing lasts forever and everything can change in an instant. One day we will be free, but until then, we need to become strong enough to be able to retain our freedom."

"Wise words."

"Thanks. So can you explain what you meant by 'short-ears' and 'druids'?"

"Right, right. In simple terms, short-ears are dirty, pink-skinned dimwits, almost the size of bugbears, whose culture can differ a lot depending on the location of their tribe. The ones we fought, called the Pallax, prefer to live near swamps and have no problem fighting naked as long as they have their bodies covered in their war paint." Ban shook his head.

"Did they attack you?" asked Gul, causing Ban to smile viciously.

"Nope. We went to their village to pay them back for stealing some pigs and roughing up a few of our men in the middle of the night."

Gul scratched his head. "Pigs?"

Ban, Gozzag, and Rogga, who was now engaged in their discussion, stopped walking and stood there shocked. Ban facepalmed and the other two hollered in laughter.

"Never mind, kid," Ban replied, wiping tears from his eyes. "Never mind! Let's get back to the story. We went there to pay them back, and pay them back we did! They might have been taller than us, but they were not as tough. We met them in open battle and managed to make them bleed. In the end, we lost two men, and they, seven."

"That doesn't seem so bad."

"It's not, and they can thank the druids for that. That weird order of short-eared philosophers and mystics boggles my mind. They act like bards and they have the same status as nobles, yet they take it upon themselves to stop wars. Why we went through all that trouble and why we should listen to them, I'll never understand..." Ban's voice trailed off.

Gozzag knocked him on the forehead. "Hey, what was that for!" Ban growled.

Gozzag glared at him. "For being an idiot. We gained four additional pigs and four sheep without many losses thanks to their intervention. Besides, they're like priests, only more fun to talk to because they're more hardworking and less entitled." Gozzag turned to Volker and Gul. "Here's a lesson for the future. In case your tribe ever regains their freedom and happens upon a tribe of those southern short-ears, respect their religions and traditions and they'll respect yours."

"Unless they're the new guys further south. You know, the ones who are wearing almost matching outfits and carrying banners everywhere they go."

Gozzag visibly cringed. "The Brizilum Republic... Yeah, they're the exception. Dirty skirt-wearers killed the druids of the Gallas, who were trying to negotiate a peaceful resolution to the conflict, with cold blood. Not to mention, they burned down the Gallas' shrines and tore down the statues of their gods. They even replaced them with their own. I'll never work for them ever again even if they offer us a mountain of gold."

"You worked for them?" Volker asked, his curiosity about the outside world surpassing his previous caution.

"Yeah. We're from a clan of mercenaries, though you probably didn't know that. The Brizilum Republic is made of warriors who fight for gold, silver, and other valuables. We fought many battles and won most of them against all odds."

Ban grinned. "We're one of the best!"

"So you're here not as slaves, but as *mercenaries*?" Volker asked, causing Ban's grin to fade and Gozzag to groan.

Gozzag cleared his throat. "Not quite. We made a blunder during our last assignment, so now we've been forced to join Bulgu's expedition. We were supposed to defend the second youngest brother during the Kur attack, but they had more men than we'd thought and they caught us off-guard. It was bad, but not the worst mistake we've made."

Ban sighed. "The worst thing was participating in the Brizilum republic's invasion on the Gallas. We only joined a few battles and trained their men a little, and you wanna know what we got in the end?"

"What?" Volker asked.

"Our reputation was ruined down south, and that's where most of the good fights that pay a lot are. I really wish we'd known they were sacrilegious assholes before accepting their offer... Why would they destroy the history of their foes?"

Volker reached a conclusion. "Wouldn't it be easy to replace the conquered people's lost culture with theirs?"

"The bastards..." muttered Gozzag.

"I don't get it," said Ban.

"Me neither," Gul added.

"They're changing the people's identity to theirs. Give it a few generations and there will be a whole new loyal Brizilum colony ready to serve the Republic," Gozzag explained.

"But that's not our problem, right? It's not like they'll spread all the way to the north. What resources could they find here? They could find much more of it in the warmer and more fertile south."

"I don't think it's about resources, Ban. Once we return, we should tell the others."

"Do you think they'll listen to mere speculation? And even if they did, we're stuck here until we finish our goal—I'm sure Bulgu wouldn't care and we can't fight our way back."

Gozzag sighed. "Dammit, you're right. But we should still tell them so someone can spread the message if we die."

"Sure, but let's talk about something else. Like the time we ambushed the Jakkar—"

Rogga interrupted Ban as he growled towards the left.

"What is it?"

"Found two Hivelings, and they've found us. They're heading towards us."

CHAPTER 19
THE HIVE'S WRATH

Everyone took Rogga's announcement differently.

Gozzag sighed, Ban grinned savagely, Rogga kept his attention on the incoming hivelings, Gul shuddered, Molg prayed, and Jag, the most average looking of Volker's party, gripped his spear tightly. Volker took a few deep breaths to steel his nerves before he blew his horn, grabbing everyone's attention.

"What was that for!" yelled Rogga.

"I was letting the other groups know that we encountered some hivelings so they can come and help us deal with them and others that may follow them later."

"While letting more of the bugs know where we are?" asked Rogga, glaring fiercely at Volker.

"Fun fact, hivelings have terrible hearing. They do have other ways to send messages, but from what our kind has observed across these years, it takes so much time for those messages to disseminate that we theorize they communicate via smells. Rogga, do you sense anything new?" Volker asked the burga.

Rogga sniffed the air. His ears twitched. "From the bugs? No, they're just standing there, but I can smell their aggression from here and... what is that other smell? Bah, who cares. The important thing is, they're going to attack once they're done with whatever they're doing." Rogga sniffed some more. "It seems you're right."

"He's right? About what?" Ban asked before the distant sound of horns entered his ears.

Volker smiled, in a way imitating Lev. "All right men, prepare formation. We'll take on one of those monsters while Gozzag and the rest take on the other. Is that acceptable?"

Gozzag shrugged. "Suits us just fine."

"What? You want us to fight?" asked Gul.

Volker looked at his friend. "Yes. Do you have a better idea?"

"Let's run for it," Gul suggested in a worried tone.

Ban laughed. "Run away? Sorry, kid. I'm not into the habit of running away from bugs."

"Not to mention, from what we've seen from the past months, they're faster than us. I'm sure that once we try to run they'll abandon what they're doing to chase after us, and you can bet that they'll catch us unprepared before we regroup with the others. Even if we throw away all our equipment; only our burga friend would be able to escape," Gozzag said while pointing at Rogga, causing him to snarl.

"I'd never run away!"

Ban laughed again. "Nobody said you would, buddy."

"Why not? No offence, but wouldn't that be the smart thing to do?" Gul asked while nervously eyeing the burga and two dekas.

Gozzag frowned, slighted by Gul's accusation. "If we were to do the smart thing, we'd leave at least two of you bogeys behind to feed the beasts. You should thank the gods that Ban and I could each take down a hiveling by ourselves, and that Rogga is a burga. It doesn't matter whether you'd call it 'logical' or 'smart' or even 'cowardly' to abandon your companions to save yourself—not a single of Rogga's kinsmen would ever back down from an opportunity to fight together to the last man, and Rogga is no different," he lectured. "Of course, if you do want us to escape, then have I got the perfect role for you!"

Gul lowered his head. "N-No, thank you, sir... and I'm sorry..."

"Just watch your tongue, kid. And instead of wasting our time talking, why don't we prepare ourselves?"

Volker patted Gul on the back. "He's right, Gul. This isn't the time for idle chatter."

"I-I know it isn't, but I just want an alternative, you know? I don't wanna get killed and eaten by giant bugs."

"Who does? Sadly, we haven't a choice but to fight," Volker responded matter-of-factly.

Gul noticed that the tips of Volker's ears were constantly twitching, which he knew happened whenever Volker was afraid. Gul wanted to ask why Volker was putting on a show of bravery, but neither of the other two bogeys were in much better shape than he. *Volker's trying to keep everyone calm,* Gul thought. *Well, if we can't run, then we can only fight. Gods, I hate fighting...*

"Well then, let's show those bugs we're not easy prey," Gul said in false bravado. Volker ordered his men to prepare for the tough battle ahead.

* * *

Everyone prayed for aid from their respective gods while they waited for the hivelings to arrive. The two dekas prayed for a valiant battle, the burga for a worthy hunt, and the bogeys for protection against the blighted beasts crawling towards them.

"Remind me again why we didn't prepare an ambush?" Jag asked Volker, shuddering. They stood in a loose three-man formation shaped like a reverse arrow consisting of Jag on the left, Volker on the right, and Molg in the centre, with Gul a short distance away to provide support with his sling.

Volker glanced at Jag. "There are only a few creatures that can conceivably ambush a hiveling, and unfortunately our kind isn't one of them."

"Great. Just great... And do you think these weird wooden spears will actually be able to kill them? Wouldn't our normal spears be better?" Jag asked, his gaze switching between his usual obsidian-headed spear that was lashed against his shield and the oddly-shaped wooden one in his hand.

After the battle against Gelmar, Lev had equipped his men with two different spears, one primary and one sidearm. The main spear was designed to be used mainly against hivelings and other large beasts, and the shorter sidearm spear to be used as a ranged weapon. The sidearm spear could have passed for a normal spear made of hardened wood if not for its barbed, detachable head, bound by a rope to the shaft.

"As long as you make sure to aim at the thing's weak points— anything showing through gaps in its shell."

"Sorry, but I regret to say I didn't pay attention when you and the boss were cutting up those things and poking their insides. I prefer to keep my lunch in my stomach."

Volker groaned. "You're saying it like we were playing around with the things. It made me sick, but we needed to see how they—"

"They're here!" Rogga roared, breaking their conversation.

Everyone turned towards the direction in which the burga was pointing. Two giant forms emerged from the distance and charged towards them, creating disturbances in the tall grass as multiple small creatures fled out of their path.

Volker shuddered but took deep breaths to calm himself. "Everyone, prepare yourselves! Gul, load the sling and wait for my signal!"

"A-Alright!" he yelled before he loaded a lead shot into the sling and began the first rotation.

Volker tightly gripped his spear and prayed, even though he was skeptical that the gods existed at all. "O Zeja, if you exist, please guide our weapons," he muttered between deep breaths while keeping his eyes locked onto the two incoming giants. He saw from this distance that they were common workers, seemingly on the smaller side. If each pair took on one, and his plan worked, it could end in a flawless victory, or at least one with minimal losses. He felt hope well up in his heart.

Volker gave a quick glance towards Gozzag's party and could see him and Ban ready for battle, with each wielding an iron-headed axe and a round iron-banded shield. He couldn't understand why they chose a fragile metal like iron instead of bronze, but now was not the time to ask. He turned his gaze towards Rogga who was a distance away dual-wielding two bronze-tipped javelin, prepared to make them fly and pierce through their foe's shell and embed in the soft flesh below.

Volker returned his gaze towards the approaching hivelings, and once they were a mere hundred meters away he shouted. "Now!"

Both Gul and Rogga launched their own attacks at the same time, each grabbing their foe's attention as the creatures separated and charged towards them.

Just as planned, the formation impeded the hiveling worker, preventing it from reaching Gul. Molg braced himself as the creature slammed into his shield, nearly knocking him backwards off his feet. Its mandibles now lodged in his shield, the thing flailed its head about, trying to yank the shield out of Molg's grip.

"Please! Take care of this thing already!" he whimpered, the worker whacking him with its front legs between flails.

"We're trying, but it's not giving us a chance!" Jag yelled before he blocked a kick from the giant insect.

"Hyuguhyuguhyugu!" It let out a shrill chirp from its abdomen before it tried to turn and slam Jag. It then tried to lunge at Volker, but Volker immediately slammed his shield into its head, disrupting its attempt before thrusting his spear towards its right eye and striking chitin.

The worker then grabbed the sides of Molg's shield with its front limbs and attempted to climb on top of it to crush him with its weight. Molg quickly let go of the shield and rolled to the left. He then rolled once again as it followed him and tried to bite his torso. He kept evading the hiveling's attacks as it locked onto him, considering him the weakest of the bunch while ignoring the rest as their wooden spears, in most cases, wouldn't be able to penetrate its armour.

The worker suddenly charged at Volker. Volker failed to evade, and the worker pinned him to the ground. Volker tried to scamper away, but the worker blocked his path with its feet. He stared at it in fear and it gazed at him with its cold compound eyes. Acidic saliva dripped from its mouth onto the ground, sizzling and melting the dirt. Volker managed to retain his spear and thrust it forwards towards the monster's right eye, only for the hiveling to block the spear with its mandibles, catching it, and snapping the shaft in half before throwing the broken parts to the side.

Volker shivered as it chirped and brushed him with its antenna. It clicked its mandibles preparing to strike. He closed his eyes. "I shouldn't be here... I shouldn't die like this... I wanna live... Mr. Gherm, Gul, guys, someone, anyone, help!"

Suddenly a loud bang rang out, and the beast screeched. Volker opened his eyes and saw that the creature's strike hadn't arrived. Instead, the hiveling worker had turned its head to the left where he saw Gul in the distance.

"You like that? How about another one!" shouted Gul. He hurled another lead shot towards the hiveling, hitting it in the thorax and cracking its shell.

Volker quickly got up and ran away. The worker turned back towards him and about to give chase, but instead shrieked in agonizing pain.

"Got ya!" Jag yelled. He yanked the spear shaft out, leaving the detached head in the right side of the worker's abdominal segment, and jumped backwards.

Still shrieking, the hiveling wiggled its abdomen, trying to get the alien object out, but the barbs on the spear-point kept it in place. Molg followed, after a delay, jamming his own spear into the hiveling's thorax.

"Spin around and tie its legs!" shouted Volker, brandishing his spear.

The two bogeys did as asked. The hiveling struggled—it could not reach the ropes even when it curled its body. It charged forward, aiming to drag and tire the two bogeys so they would release the ropes, but it could not maintain its balance as it kept getting pulled from both directions. Once its legs tangled with the ropes, it stumbled and fell to the ground.

As it was trying to untangle its feet and stand up, Volker lunged and stabbed it in the head.

The hiveling let out a terrible cry and thrashed around, but Volker kept hold of his spear. "Stab it now!" he roared.

Molg and Jag approached and stabbed it with their standard spears, one in the bottom of the head and the other in the middle of the thorax, causing it to struggle more violently as a beast in its death throes. They then took out their shorter spears and stabbed it once again. The beast thrashed less and less, until it finally stopped entirely.

"It's over..." Molg muttered exhaustedly before sitting down on the ground.

"No, it's not. We have to help Gozzag and the others deal with the other one," Volker said before searching for their companions. In the end, he found a shocking scene.

Molg rubbed his eyes. "It doesn't look like they need our help."

Gozzag's party had chopped the other hiveling into multiple pieces. The head, along with the legs, was lying on the ground in a pool of bluish-green hemolymph. All of the dismembered body parts were covered with serious injuries, especially the abdomen which had more than six javelins stuck piercing through the shell.

Volker turned to their companions. They had suffered only a few minor injuries.

"Nice job!" yelled Ban as he approached with a grin on his face.

"Thanks. Looks like you're alright yourselves."

"Yeah. It was a good exercise." Ban's words caused everyone to flinch. Who would take fighting giant beasts as an exercise?

Gozzag swaggered over. "From the looks on your faces, I can tell what you're all thinking. But remember that these two were smaller compared to the norm and honestly, dumber too. If we'd fought a weaker but smarter and less predictable foe, I can assure you that nobody would be smiling."

Volker nodded. "Alright, now that's settled, can you ask Rogga if any more hivelings are coming?"

"We already did. Three more are coming, but they won't be here before our reinforcements. They'll be easy pickings."

"Do we know who's coming?"

Ban turned to Rogga's general direction. "Hey, Rogga! Who was it again?" he yelled.

"A few bogeys and a party of goblins! One smells like a female!" Rogga yelled back.

Volker thought about the information. "Goblins that are actually doing something and are led by a female..." He rubbed his forehead. "It's Rapha, isn't it?"

"Yup," Ban said with a grin.

"Wonderful..."

* * *

For as long as Rapha could remember, nothing had gone well for her. She was born to the Ajiin, one of the "dim" goblin clans who'd migrated from the north-eastern lands. Because the Ajiin had not been "enlightened" by Ainshart, the Jiira and other descendants of Ainshart's once-great kingdom considered the Ajiin "dim." Once the local tribes discovered that the Ajiin were too powerful to be conquered, that idea lost traction; as it turned out, all Ajiin, no matter their status and gender, were born with a weapon in hand and were trained their entire lives for blood and battle.

Rapha should have been a mother, or better yet, a war-maiden. A beacon of fear for the people of these lands as they looked out of their dwellings. Alas, a long time ago in a drunken stupor, her father Hijmald had chopped off the chief's son's left hand for protecting his sister when Hijmald had tried to seduce her. This matter had been taken to the high council, the Otum, which had decided that not only did Hijmald have to pay thirty golden Karls, but that he also had to chop off his own left hand.

This obviously hadn't sat well with the fool, so he had opted to issue a duel of storms to the chief instead. And so, he'd fought the chief on a narrow wooden platform above a pit full of spikes, during a heavy storm, under the gaze of the four gods.

Rapha bit her lip as she remembered how her father had fallen to his death, impaled in the shark wooden spikes. How his eyes searched for salvation, left and right, only to lose their light as his cries for help slowly turned into gurgles of blood, before ending in silence.

Then had come their turn. Per the rules of the duel of storms, the victor could dictate the fate of the loser's family. It usually ended in either death or enslavement for three generations, but thankfully the chief had decided to exile them instead. Despite his grievances with her father, the chief had already settled the score and was not the type to take his anger out on women and children.

His family, and a few of the other houses were of a different mind though, so he had believed that exile would both appease his kin and protect Rapha's family from them. Sadly, fellow clansmen hadn't been the only threat. Rapha, her mother, and her paternal uncle who had joined them to pay for his brother's foolishness, had soon encountered a Jiira war band returning from battle. Needless to say, it hadn't ended well...

They had tried to resist, but it had all been in vain. Her uncle was slain after killing three men, while she and her mother were captured and separated after they were appraised in the Jiira's town. Her mother, who was fairly fit but not athletic, was sent to "the house of desires" to serve as a prostitute, while she, who had trained and aspired to become a war-maiden, was sent to serve as a harem guard.

"Is everything alright? Still thinking about the past?" interrupted Ruune, her second in command. The two had served in the harem guard together and had become close friends since.

"Thinking more about how we got in this situation," replied Rapha before ducking under another branch. She was getting sick of the sixth floor and its jungle-like environment.

"Well, it's all a certain fat bastard's fault," said Ruune in a hushed tone before taking a glance at the nearby hand carriage carrying Bulgu. "Sometimes I don't know what's worse, serving in the old chief's harem guards or serving Bulgu."

"They're both bad. Both of them are a joke, and you can tell that by what we're wearing." Rapha's armour—if it deserved to be called that— was the same design as the harem guards' armour, but blue instead of the usual red. It consisted of an artistically crafted ceremonial chest plate that foolishly left the abdomen exposed, gaudy boots unsuitable for marching, and a small plate over the hips, covered by a flowy short skirt.

Ruune sighed. "These outfits just show that we're nothing more than decorations in his eyes. We're not amazingly beautiful decorations either, apparently. Once the fat bastard realized how truly dangerous this place is, he threw us on grunt duty."

"At least they *look* good," Rapha said sarcastically causing Ruune to giggle.

"According to Bulgu's standards," Ruune said with a smile. "Never lose that sense of humour, Rapha. Life would be dull without it."

"Will do, though I bet I can be a bit more humorous once we get out of these damn woods."

Ruune frowned. "I wouldn't count on that. I heard the next floor is way worse."

"Of course it is... why wouldn't it be. That's what we need, right? More death and more bugs..."

"At least we found some reliable company." Ruune pointed at the formation which consisted of greyborn bogeys. Most of them, with a few exceptions, were unruly and shivering as they huddled together, afraid of the unknown. But even within the exceptions, a single squad stood out. They marched confidently in their matching gear, a spear in their right hands and a marching pack slung atop their left shoulders. The red eye in the centres of their wooden shields seemed to glow as they hung from the men's right shoulders.

Rapha frowned. "Reliable, yes. Trustworthy, no."

"I don't understand what you've got against them. From what we've seen, they're disciplined and versatile, *and* they've had our backs whenever we've had any trouble. Sure, we saved Volker less than a month ago, but they've been pretty nice to us."

Rapha sighed. "A little too nice, you mean? I just can't seem to trust their leader. I keep feeling like there's something wrong about him. My guts tell me he's a snake."

Ruune looked towards Lev. As always, he was discussing some matters with Volker, Jem, and some other members of his group. "Can't see what you hate about him. There's nothing wrong with a leader who informs his men of his plan and takes their advice seriously."

"I feel he's more of a manipulator than a leader. He has the smell of an elder of the Otum... One who's more of a merchant than a warrior."

"What? Haven't you seen him fight?"

"I did see him. But that's why it makes even less sense. How many warriors have we seen fight with words and swords as well as he does?"

"I don't know. You're the expert in these things. You know I used to guard pigs at night in my village's farm before this— Duck!" An unidentifiable projectile whizzed over their heads.

"I hate this forest."

"We all do."

As they walked, they heard one of the nearby burga growl.

"What is it?" Rapha asked.

"Something smells... wrong," the burga replied.

"How far?"

The burga sniffed the air, ears twitching. Suddenly his eyes widened. "Above us!" An unidentified scream came from the back.

Rapha looked behind her and saw a green bogey tangled by a yellowish thread before being lifted up in the air.

"What the fuck is that?!" Ruune asked as she saw a giant brownish-green insect with six long thin legs, two yellow eyes, and two fuzzy antennas feasting upon one of the vanguard members. The figure stared at them while dragging the man, using the thread hanging from a pouch, under its mandibles, closer to its mouth.

"Hivelings!" yelled another warrior.

Lovely! We've got spiders, too? Rapha squeaked to herself.

Hivelings were known to come in various shapes, but the spider form was one of the rarest. They were commonly found in the lower floors, and this jungle-like floor was quite hospital to them—spider-form hivelings could use the abundance of thick branches to manoeuvre.

The creature grinded its plates and emitted a horrible chirping sound before ten more sets of eyes started to glow. In quick succession, the area was filled with a chorus of chirps, cancelling out most of the natural sounds that were familiar to this jungle floor.

"Javelins! Kill those things, now!" yelled one of Bulgu's men.

"What a fool," Rapha said as she saw them throw their javelins at targets far too high up in the trees to reach. Rapha brought out her shortsword and took out a red-eyed shield she had borrowed from one of Lev's men after its owner had died a week ago. "Get into formation!" she yelled. Her squad hoisted their shields above them, forming a barrier, and braced themselves for impact.

Before the other men could grab their weapons, the hivelings dropped down en masse and began clawing at their goblinoid enemies. Most of Rapha's men, nearly empty-handed, defended themselves as best they could from the incoming barrage of swift attacks.

The creature slashed at the wooden wall, trying to break through to the prey beneath. The armour on its limbs was lighter than the average hiveling, so Rapha and the rest baited it by leaving an opening in their shield wall. Once the spider-like hiveling extended its limbs through the opening, the spear-wielders pinned them to the ground using their bronze-headed spears.

"Kill it!" Rapha yelled. They dragged the creature down onto the ground before releasing a merciless barrage of attacks on the wailing beast. It tried to fight back, but only managed to injure the exposed abdomen of a single harem guard before Rapha stabbed it in the head, covering her in the creature's yellowish blood—which, to her surprise, was not corrosive.

"I *really* hate this armour," Rapha growled.

"Got one. Six more to go," Ruune panted.

"Only six more, huh? Who has the most kills?"

"It's a tie between Lev's group and the dekas— oh, wait, Lev's in the lead with three kills."

Rapha smiled. "Not bad. Let's try our best as well. We have to make sure these fuckers pay for killing one of us. Another one, incoming!" she belted out. "Prepare fo... for..." Her voice trailed off. She stumbled and fell to the ground.

"Rapha!" Ruune screamed. She saw a few other warriors fall to the ground, all of whom were covered with yellowish blood.

"What's going on?" Thought Rapha as she tried, to no avail, stand up. She glanced at her surroundings before she noticed movement in the nearby bushes. A few tiny, spider-like hivelings emerged and covered her with their threads. They then tried to drag her away while the other guards dealt with the bigger hivelings.

"No..." she thought before losing consciousness.

APHA

RAK

LEV
(Gherm)

CHAPTER 20

YELLOW BLOOD

"Uuugh," groaned Rapha. Her vision was blurry and her head felt like it was going to split in half. She tried to massage her forehead, but to her surprise, her arms were tightly bound to her torso in a cocoon.

"I would stop struggling so much if I were you," said a somewhat familiar, masculine voice from her left.

"I'd agree with the lad. The last thing we need is to anger these foul creatures a second time," sighed an older and gruffer voice.

"Who're you? Where are we?" asked Rapha.

"What's the last thing you remember?" asked a younger fellow in kind.

"We were ambushed by spider-like hivelings... And I, with the rest of the harem guards managed to take down one... Then I fell on the ground and passed out..."

"Pfff! Only one?" laughed a third voice to her right. She glared at the large blurry figure.

"How many did *you* kill?"

"Well, last I'd checked, Lev over there killed four, I killed three, Rak killed three, and this piece of shit here... also killed three."

"You're such an amiable fellow, Hemgall."

"Shut it, Vyrga," Hemgall growled.

"Charming, aren't you? That's just what I'd expect from one of Rak's pets."

"It's called loyalty, you wretched pig!"

"A meaningless concept meant to tame fools. It's only ever a matter of time until self-interest compels you."

"Well, I'm compelled to rip a hole in your guts!"

"You wish, you dirty mutt."

As they continued throwing insults at each other, Rapha turned towards the only individual she knew among the crowd.

"So even you're here, Lev."

As her vision cleared, she recoiled a bit at his smug expression.

"I would have preferred not."

"That's one thing we can all agree on," Hemgall replied in her stead.

"I concur," Vyrga said with a frown.

Rapha sighed. "Looks like we'll all die here, right?"

"I doubt that," Lev replied.

"How so?" asked Rapha.

"Guess. Better yet, look. Even if everything is blurry, isn't there something missing? And isn't there something weird happening around you?"

The place was dark, though a few luminescent shapes here and there emitted soft white light. There was no greenery, but there were weird forms floating about, three of them resembling hivelings.

Vyrga sighed. "If intellectuals like you all haven't guessed yet, then I fear for the future of our races. And before you open your mouth, Hemgall, we're on the seventh floor."

Vyrga's announcement shocked everyone except Lev.

"It can't be—" Hemgall muttered.

"But it is, Hem. We're too deep to be rescued. Yes, we're not dead, but we may be soon. Those bugs must be preparing something—why else would they bring us here?"

Hemgall shook his head. "There's no way they're that smart. They might be able to ambush us from time to time, but any creature with strong instincts could do that."

"Would a creature with 'strong instincts' figure out, in its own short lifespan, how to deceive the burgas' senses and strategically target half, if not most of, its enemies' leaders? We've been underestimating the hivelings. Vyrga and I believe their attack was coordinated. Unless you have a better idea as to why we're stuck here."

"That's because... it's... dammit, you're right," Hemgall admitted.

Vyrga smirked. "He is, isn't he?" He turned towards Lev. "So, Lev, how do we get out of here?"

Lev raised an eyebrow. "You're awfully nice today."

"To avoid death, I can be the nicest man in the world. Make no mistake. I won't surrender my soul to it until the time is right."

"When would that be?"

Vyrga would have shrugged if he could. "When I fulfil my desires and I'm satisfied with the way the world is."

"So never."

Vyrga chuckled. "Who knows? My desires don't matter to the world, but I will force my will on it until I'm unable to do so anymore. Now tell us, what's your plan?"

"The paralysis has worn off and your vision has stabilized, right?"

"Yes?"

"Too bad, since this means you'll see and feel everything they'll do later."

"What? You mean—"

Lev threw his arms up in resignation. "I have no plan."

His party was speechless. Rapha cried, Hemgall cursed, and Vyrga doubted.

Hemgall was the first to talk again. "So we're doomed, huh?"

"Looks like it. At least we've got time for one last thing," Lev replied, looking in Vyrga's direction.

"And what is this 'last thing'?" Hemgall pressed.

"Before the spiderlings come for us, you can settle the score."

"Spiderlings?"

"They're basically spider hivelings, so spiderlings."

"Oh. Wait, settle what score?"

"I thought you'd enjoy bashing Vyrga's head in for what he said about you and your family while you were out."

"What!" Hemgall seethed.

Vyrga's eyes widened. "What are you saying, Lev? Why would I sully my tongue by mentioning the ilk of this drooling dog?"

"Because you're that kinda guy, you filthy bastard" Hemgall shouted. "If you have something to say to me, say it to my face!"

"You couldn't even count the number of the things I dislike about you, you irredeemable cur."

"I'm sure you'd rather go play your sad little flute like always!" Hemgall spat. "If I could use my arms, I'd—"

Vyrga headbutted his adversary.

"Owww!" Hemgall howled.

Though Vyrga's mouth was smiling, his eyes were not. "You went too far, whelp. I'm not going to need arms for what I'm about to do to you."

"Neither am I!" Hemgall growled.

The two began to brawl, and just as Lev had predicted, they drew the attention of the three hivelings. "Rapha, keep an eye out in case any other threats appear," he requested in a low voice.

"Why?" she rasped.

"Because I'm going to get us out. I had a spare knife around, but I needed a distraction."

Rapha assented. All three insects were occupied trying to paralyze the brawlers.

She heard a soft sawing noise followed by a snap. After making a hole in his cocoon, Lev cut the rest of himself free and fell to the floor.

The sound of his landing caught the hivelings' attention, but by the time they had turned towards him, he had already freed Rapha.

Lev put his hands on Rapha's shoulders. "Can you still fight?"

"You're not running away?" she asked.

"Where would I?" Lev suddenly grabbed her by the arm and dragged her away. Before she could complain, she heard a loud crash behind her and stone fragments rained in the vicinity. When she looked behind her, she found the largest of the three hivelings staring at them and the other two floating around.

"What's... What's going on?"

"Seventh floor. That's what's going on. You haven't done any research, have you? This place defies the laws of physics."

"'Physics?'"

"The laws of this world. On the seventh floor, there are places where the force holding us down to the ground, also known as gravity, is stronger, and in other places it's non-existent. Seems like hivelings are used to this kind of environment."

"So what should we do?"

"Boost our numbers. I distract the hivelings and try to free those two while you release the other captives. I've already scouted the areas where gravity changes. And before you ask, no, I'm not sure I can take both hivelings on. But we don't have a choice, so go."

Rapha nodded and quickly moved to perform her task. She brought out a secondary sword that she had strapped to the back of her waist in case of emergencies. It had maddened her that she had been unable to grab it when she was restrained.

She reached the first cocoon on her right and proceeded to slice it open. Out fell a deka, onto his knees. He took a couple of deep breaths before yelling, "What the fuck's going on?"

"A fight! Get up!" Rapha helped him to his feet.

The confused deka looked about and saw Lev, who was armed with a short spear, getting tackled by a hiveling in the air "Bugs! Again? And since when can they and bogeys fly!"

"Since now! Move it!" Rapha growled as she shoved the man forward.

"Okay, okay! What a bitch!" The deka growled as he grabbed his sword and charged forward.

Rapha ignored his insult and continued freeing captives left and right, until they reached eighteen in total. She then turned and joined the battle herself.

The hivelings had also bolstered their numbers and had now become twelve. Eight drones, three spiderlings—and a warrior.

"Gods, no," she muttered. The behemoth, clicking its mandibles, gazed down at them from the ceiling with its menacing compound eyes. Everyone nervously awaited the giant behemoth to join the battle, and once the other hivelings had worn out the men by sacrificing five of their own, the warrior made its move. It floated slowly towards them, but in the blink of an eye, the surrounding air glimmered, and the giant slammed into the ground, sending out a shockwave. Rapha managed to grab a stalagmite to steady herself, but half of her fellow captives were not so lucky. Only Hemgall, Vyrga, Lev, the two dekas, and the darg managed to keep their footing.

The hivelings used this opportunity to charge at the goblinoids. They attacked from both land and air, but the goblinoids refused to back down. Nobody wanted to be devoured by the beasts, and as there was no way out, they fought as hard as they could, swords, axes, and knives against claws and mandibles. Cries of war from men who wanted to live combined cacophonously with dreadful screeches from beasts who wanted to devour them.

Just as a brown bogey wielding a flimsy stone knife was about to suffer a killing blow from a drone, Rapha charged and slashed at the creature's eye, forcing it to back away from its prey.

"Get up! I'm not fighting this thing on my own!" she growled. She kept her eyes on the hiveling while helping him up, but as soon as he returned to his feet, he shoved Rapha towards the hiveling.

"Forgive me, but I have a family!" he said before running away.

"What—coward!" she roared. She tried to roll out of the hiveling's way, only to be knocked back down by the drone. She then tried to roll away from the creature, but it stomped on her left arm, crushing her bones.

"Aaaaargh!" she screamed. The weight of the beast bore down on her arm. When she tried to slash at it with her other arm, the hiveling ripped the sword from her hand by the blade and threw it to the side.

"No. Not like this! Someone help!" she yelled as the drone lowered its head towards her neck, clicking nonstop. She thrashed and struggled; it crushed her other arm. Her screams heightened to a pitch she never knew she could reach.

Her vision spotty, she looked around for salvation. Everyone else was occupied.

"Please... Someone help," she choked through tears as the hiveling scrutinized her with its empty yellow eyes. It clicked its mandibles one last time before everything was covered in blood—yellow blood.

The hiveling screeched as it received a spear to the upper corner of its right eye. Suddenly it released her and started bucking uncontrollably. There was a grey bogey riding on its neck joint and repeatedly stabbing it with an onyx knife.

The hiveling bucked and rolled, threatening to crush her until two grey hands dragged her away.

"Got her, kid!" she heard a voice say before she passed out.

* * *

"Got her, kid!" yelled Hemgall as he dragged Rapha away from the hiveling.

"Damn! Done with Vyrga already?" Lev roared. With all his might, he popped the head of the hiveling off its body and hurled it to the ground. The head clicked its mandibles a couple of times before its eyes lost their light.

"One more drone down. Just a spiderling and a warrior to go," Hemgall said before he looked towards the giant behemoth that was fighting two dekas, two burgas, and three goblins in close range while another three upper-class bogeys, who were gifted in magic, along with Vyrga, who was wielding a bow, were providing ranged support. The remaining three surviving greyborn bogeys gathered around Lev and Hemgall.

"Settling the score can wait. I still can't believe that such ungrateful shits exist," Hemgall growled as he looked towards the previous green bogey's corpse.

"What'd you expect from someone who'd never fought for his life before?" Lev asked.

"Something more honourable, at least."

"No offence, but honour won't help much when you're dead."

"Then why didn't you leave her to die?"

"I have my reasons." Lev smiled. "Let's talk later. We have some hivelings to take care of."

"Sure. Can't let that shitbag take all the credit," Hemgall replied with a smile.

"Then let's go. We'll deal with the drones and the spiderling, then we'll join the attack on the warrior."

Hemgall readied his axe. He was itching to make the hivelings pay.

"You're guarding her, by the way," Lev interrupted.

"Oh, come on!" Hemgall whined. "Why me? And who told you you could order me around!"

What do you suggest then? Leave her alone?"

"No, you guard her while I take care of the big guy. You know I'm the most battle-hardened bogey here—it would be a waste for me to stay back. Besides, you're the leader-ish type of guy, so it's best for you to maintain order while battle-maniacs like me deal with the bloody part."

Lev shrugged. "If you insist. If you die, don't blame me."

"Don't worry, I won't."

Lev watched Hem and the rest leave as he sat next to the unconscious girl.

He smiled. "That's one way to avoid dying, I guess." Lev had predicted that they would be able to take the behemoth down, but not without heavy losses; this time, even with his help, they wouldn't be able to mitigate their losses by much. He was planning to interfere when the time was right, but for now, he chose to wait, wait for the moment to strike. Besides, he truly wanted to help the girl despite her wariness towards him. She would be a vital source of information about the world outside the cave—she was too valuable to die.

Hemgall breathed heavily, his body covered in bleeding lacerations as he glared at the hiveling warrior as it was about to launch its next move.

"Out of the way!" Hemgall yelled as the hiveling warrior charged towards them. He rolled out of the way and evaded being crushed by the behemoth. When he looked back, he saw three more victims added to its kill count. Two greyborns and a goblin had been crushed under the beast's feet. Half of their bodies had been turned to mush while the other half continued to wriggle about.

"Hey, weren't you asses supposed to provide us support? Where's your fancy magic now?"

"We're working on it, greyborn! Magic is neither easy nor fast!" yelled a green bogey, pointing her focus, in the form of an amulet, at the hiveling. She tightened her grip and chanted faster and faster. Moments later, an energy bolt shot out of the focus into the hiveling, but did little more than dent its carapace.

"Wow, so powerful," mocked one deka, drawing the shamans' indignation.

Hemgall could not believe his luck. He was stuck battling a giant insectoid monster with a bunch of barely competent fools; in his eyes, the only other individuals here who were worthy of respect were Lev, the darg, and unfortunately Vyrga. Whether it was a miracle or dumb luck, he was thankful that they had managed to deal with all the other beasts, saving this giant for last.

The hiveling warrior was about to charge once again, but it cancelled its attack after receiving a copper arrow to its left eye which caused it to screech and turn towards the attacker, Vyrga. *At least that bastard is doing something right,* Hemgall thought before running and sliding under the hiveling's legs.

He hacked away at the unarmoured portions of its legs with his axe, causing it to switch its attention to him. It tried to crouch to crush him with its weight, but he managed to roll out before it landed.

As the hiveling turned towards Hemgall, he stood up and raised his axe. "Come on! Show me what you've got!"

The hiveling clicked and twirled its antenna in response before turning just a bit to the left and charging in that direction, towards a wall and chasm leading deeper into the abyss. Hemgall wondered why it was not charging directly at him, but once it touched the wall, everything clicked.

"Get out of the way!" yelled the darg.

Hemgall immediately rolled out of the way. His foe reached the wall, rebounded off of it, shimmered a little and floated before slamming into the ground onto where he was standing.

The hiveling immediately stood up and charged head-on at Hemgall again. He tried to sidestep the attack but the hiveling suddenly turned and slammed him with its mandibles. Hemgall collided with a stalagmite, ripping it from the ground.

"Uuugh," Hemgall groaned before spitting out some blood along with a tooth. Near the hiveling distracted by shamans and a team of close combatants, he saw his axe, too far away and in too dangerous a location for him to grab. He got up and cracked his neck back into place before grabbing the broken stalagmite like a club.

This isn't enough, Hemgall thought. The stalagmite was too heavy and poorly balanced to be used offensively.

He looked at his surroundings trying to find something better. *Nothing but floating rocks around here— wait, they're floating!* With a savage grin, he jumped towards the hovering rocks and found himself released from the bounds of gravity.

He tied his improvised club to his belt, grabbed a few rocks, and immediately advanced towards the behemoth by monkey-swinging, or perhaps pulling, on the nearby stalactites. Every few pulls, he let loose a few rocks and avoided the space where they fell. He kept doing that until he was above the hiveling who just killed a goblin and was about to finish off the darg.

He grabbed the stone club and with a great roar, he jumped from the ceiling towards the unsuspecting beast and slammed its head to the ground as gravity took hold.

The hiveling screeched as it bled hemolymph. The top of its head armour had cracked.

As it shook left and right, disoriented, Hemgall kept smashing it on the head till the stalagmite broke. He jumped off and grabbed his axe.

"Now! Kill it while it's dazed!" Hemgall roared before sliding below the hiveling and slicing at its legs once more.

Lev was watching the battle. Rapha lay unconscious next to him on the ground, a wadded-up cloth supporting her head.

"Looks like it'll end soon," he said to unhearing ears as Hemgall and the other fighters lopped off the hiveling's other front leg, causing it to not only lose one of its weapons but also to have a hard time balancing the front end of its body, hurting its movement.

The hiveling grew more erratic as it tried to fend off its foes, but it was continuously pushed back without being able to inflict another major wound on one of its targets. It at last tried to escape towards the chasm.

While the shamans raised the stone in front of it to block its path, Hemgall and the rest attacked its back legs and took out the left one, crippling it and sending it to the ground, unable to move. Seemingly sensing its end, it used its central legs to quickly turn and swipe at its opponents with its head and abdomen.

The goblinoids managed to evade the swipe attack. It opened its mandibles and used its remaining strength to lunge forward, putting extreme stress on its middle legs and snapping the greyborn in front of it in half. Bound by its jaws, the bogey was frozen in shock until he realized that he was cut in half. He screamed in agony, crying and cursing before the hiveling slammed him on the bloody ground, cracking his skull.

While he was watching this scene, Lev noticed Rapha stir on the ground.

"W-What h-h-hah— raaargh!" Rapha screamed in pain.

Lev immediately grabbed a clay bottle of mushroom mead mixed with crom powder—a known fast-acting sedative Rogg had provided after a few favours—and forced a spoonful into Rapha's mouth. She choked and sputtered from the vile tasting substance. He patted her back as she coughed and cursed before slowly losing consciousness and passing out.

"Well, that's one problem delayed," Lev muttered with a look of pity as he stared at the unconscious girl. "This world isn't kind to the disabled." He contemplated the girl's future. She might be a goblin, but from what he observed, she was neither high in the Jiira social ladder nor indispensable to the expedition. It would be hard to convince her superiors to heal her.

"So Rapha—well, I suppose it's meaningless to tell you this since you're out of it. I'm going to try to squeeze out a favour from an outcast healer. They're hard to find, they only accept payment in haze crystals, and aren't that powerful or they wouldn't have been thrown aside. It'll cost you more than info and it'll take a long time for you to heal. I thoroughly expect your gratitude." He turned his gaze back to the battle to witness its end.

The once-formidable behemoth, whose kind had terrorized the expedition, now lay limbless on the ground, wailing pitifully as twelve of the fourteen remaining goblinoids hacked at its carapace and dismembered it slowly while making sure to keep it alive out of spite.

If they would only cackle madly and froth at the mouth, Lev thought, *this scene would make a great historical painting of savages.*

As the warrior let out one last wail and its eyes dimmed, he got up and carried Rapha in a princess carry. "Time to meet up with our companions."

"So the coward's here," grumbled the deka before Hem smacked him in the face, knocking him to the ground. "What was that for!"he yelled.

"Call him a coward again and our friend here won't be the only one I rip to pieces," Hem growled. The deka lowered his head.

"Not to mention that he and the lady in his grasp are our benefactors," Vyrga remarked. *Just this once, I'll let you off the hook for earlier*, he thought.

"If it wasn't for them, we would've stayed stuck in those cocoons until we became bug food," said the darg with a look of disgust.

"Who asked you, you purple sex slave! Shouldn't you be in the eastern lands crawling under a pink's feet, ready to stuff your head in their crotch?" yelled the deka before he got kicked in the nether regions by the purple man.

The darg wiped his sandals on the floor as if he was cleaning them from something dirty before he spat near the fallen buffoon, causing him to flinch. "I was a gladiator before this, you red bastard, and a great sailor before that. I don't know what you hear about my kind in your lands, but I'm a proud seaman from the prosperous state of Edoros on the fertile coast. I am a master of the white sea."

The deka sneered while standing up. "Former masters, you mean. Your people are now vassals to those new invading pinks."

"Yours will soon follow if all dekas are like you."

The deka laughed. "I wish all of them were like me! If they were, there wouldn't be cowards afraid of some fancy-dressed pinks like Gozzag and Ban! But don't worry, I'm Drogg Grimmerson! And after I defeat my brothers and inherit my father's position, I'll make sure that there won't be any more weaklings amongst my people!"

Hem, Vyrga, and Lev exchanged glances. They each had drawn the same conclusion: this Drogg needed to be disposed of, and soon, but not now while they were still in danger.

"Will she be alright?" asked the darg, ignoring the red deka's ramblings about how all those who wronged him would pay once he rose to glory.

"I was about to splint her arms, though I doubt it would make a difference," Lev admitted. "Without magical interference, it'll be a miracle if she can ever use her arms again." He gently put her down on the ground and began the operation.

"So she'll be crippled? That'll be the end for her," the darg said.

"Don't worry. I'll take care of it if we get out of here. Well, I'll try."

"I hope you do. We owe our lives to you two. I heard what happened earlier, and I have to thank you, Lev."

"No problem. By the way, I haven't gotten your name."

"Shahn Kafar, son of Kafar Ramun, at your service." The darg bowed.

"It's a pleasure." Lev bowed in reciprocity. "By the way, is there a way to shut him up?" Lev asked as he finished setting up the splints.

"It'll be an epic for the ages! The epic of the mighty Drogg, king of kings! I'll have the entire world under my people and we will!" The delusional deka kept spouting off, and Hemgall seemed ready to throw him to the dark abyss just to shut him up.

"I wish. My men and I have worked with the dekas before. There were some reasonable and respectable members, and then there was a minority of people like... that."

"These lands will bow to me!" the deka continued, unfazed. "I will engrave my name among the gods' and I will— what are you growling for, you two beasts!"

"Fool! More of them are coming!" Vyrga cut in.

"From where?" Lev responded, to Drogg's chagrin.

Suddenly, swarms of hivelings were crawling down the walls. The painfully loud din of hiveling screeches shook the foundations of the stone and forced everyone to cover their ears or risk going deaf.

"What... was that!" yelled Hemgall before the room was engulfed in purple light.

"I believe it is that," Vyrga said as he pointed at the source of the light. It was a winged purple hiveling, larger than a drone but smaller than a warrior, surrounded by an entourage of warriors. The purple hiveling opened its large, magnificent wings and they seemed to shine even further as it emitted another screech, forcing everyone to their knees.

"Aaagh! Make it stop!" cried the deka.

As though on command, the purple hiveling halted its approach. Shortly afterward, the rest of the hivelings recommenced their forward movement.

"Tch," spat Lev. "Too many hivelings, not enough morale. Great. Just great."

* * *

In the darkest depths of the abyss, in a place untouched by goblinoids and unclaimed by hivelings, a hiveling corpse lay on the hard ground. Its scarred form was broken and limbless; its cracked shell, oozing its yellowish nectar of life. Other than the corpse, there was no movement in the area until a certain bogey, lying in the centre of the beast, twitched.

"Ugh... What happened? And why is it so dark?" Lev mumbled as he touched cold chitin. "Wait. Am I sitting on a dead warrior?"

Lev suddenly remembered that he had smuggled a couple of haze crystals inside his pack. "Where's my marching pack?" he yelled as he felt around frantically for his marching pack.

He touched something warm and soft. He immediately pulled back his hand and drew his knife, trying to detect any movement in his surroundings. He picked up on a few feminine groans and the sound of laboured breathing.

"Rapha?" he asked, half-expecting a response. Lev warily pointed his knife in the direction of the sounds. He was prepared to face some kind of predatory, or at least threatening, creature capable of mimicking sounds, but after a breath, he lowered the knife. *If there were such a creature,* he realized, *it would have targeted me earlier when I was unconscious.*

Judging from the absence of light—which precluded the growth of plants—anything that lived here would be not only a blind scavenger, but also not picky enough to ignore a free meal. On the other hand, it could have eaten one of the others...

Never mind, there would've been some kind of sound if that were the case, Lev deduced. *As far as I know, everyone smuggled a few crystals, so Rapha must've kept some on her. Looks like I'll have to risk it.*

He cautiously approached the source of the noise, knowing full well he was unlikely to prevail if it struck back, and prodded it with the back of his knife. He perceived no reaction; he proceeded to touch it. *Seems like it is Rapha. Thankfully she hasn't woken up yet.* He moved his hand to the left and grazed the smooth metal of her boots—if she had been conscious, she would most likely have kicked him. *Now, if I were Rapha, where would I store those crystals?*

By the faintest reflection of light from his own eyes, Lev could just barely make out the worn straps of a backpack lying among the leftover rubble. He recognised it the instant he saw the red ribbon sticking out behind the edge of a fallen stalagmite. He remembered how most of the harem guards had used these reflective ribbons before to quickly find their equipment in low-light conditions. Lev manoeuvred around the rubble to locate the source of the reflection.

He dug his hands deep into the backpack for the crystals. *Dammit! Not here either?* he cursed to himself. He sighed and closed it, but another idea struck him. He grabbed the bag again and ran his fingers up and down the seams—some were looser than they should have been. He quickly tore apart the loosest seam, uncovering a pocket from which he plucked out a small, glowing pouch.

Bingo, he almost whispered, grabbing the haze crystal from the bag when he felt a heavy presence inside of him emanating disgust.

There you are, Gherm, he scoffed in his mind. *You haven't been active lately, so I assumed you were gone.*

Traitor... said the foreign voice in his mind.

Hey, now, I'm just doing everything I can to ensure we survive.

Shameless... fragments... within your soul... can't hide... your past, replied the voice.

Well, shame is only a concern if you live to experience it, and you can rest assured that it would be easy for me to handle something as measly as "shame." If you can't bring yourself to appreciate my experience, I can't possibly expect you to understand me, appreciate my decisions.

Broken... all of you... broken...

Lev was now quite peeved. *The sad truth is, we're all broken on the inside, but only a smart few like me realize it. You have access to my memories, so you should know this about me or—wait.* His thoughts betrayed his deepening condescension. *Did you skip the important parts because they were too much for you?* he jeered.

Gherm said, or rather thought, nothing.

Good. It's easier for you to keep your sense of self that way. Lev exhaled. *Sure, I'm more broken than the average citizen, but thankfully, unlike others in my previous line of work, I haven't hit rock bottom yet. I at least try to change things for the better.*

Not... by much...

Still, not much is better than nothing.

You're... unstable...

Lev shrugged. *True, but we can talk about my mental instability later, once we're not in danger. For now, we have more important things to do, alright?*

Gherm again thought nothing.

I'll take that as a yes. Lev returned the pouch to Rapha's backpack. He picked his new source of light back up. *Now how did we end up here?*

From what he could see, there was nothing but dirt and stones nearby. No grass, no insects, nor any other kind of fauna or flora were visible. It seemed as if the place was absorbing light—a crystal of this size and radiance should have illuminated everything within a wider radius, but here it could only shed light upon a short few killigs.

He raised the crystal to the ceiling. Light reflected and refracted off of a grey, jellylike substance. *Huh... Guess that's how we weren't reduced to paste.*

Lev lowered his guard and thought back on what happened before he woke up. *Hmm... We finished off the hiveling warrior, the dim-witted deka started an argument, and then a swarm of hivelings appeared, led by a purple one— ah, that's right!* he recalled. *We realized we couldn't handle the swarm, so before the hivelings could reach us, we dragged the carcass to the edge and held on to it tightly as we threw ourselves into the abyss.* He crossed his legs contentedly.

But... it's strange. Nobody said a word about this plan, yet we all cooperated... Why? Lev contemplated. *And how come the others aren't here?*

A feeling of warmth caressed his mind.

"Come..."

"What was th—" Lev tried to protest, but the comforting warmth was becoming hard to ignore.

"Come..."

"It must be a trap..."

"Come..."

But why does it feel so... nice? he thought. He felt warm and secure as if he were a child in his mother's lap. *Maybe it isn't a... trap...*

Lev looked towards his left. Something told him there was a path there leading to everlasting joy and happiness.

It is! Gherm shrieked, having reemerged in Lev's mind.

I know. Even if it feels nice, it's... obviously a trap. Lev took a step towards the path. *It revealed itself... when it tried to... show me a path of happiness. There's no... such thing.*

"Come!"

Shut up... Only a fool would fall for this. Lev took another step.

"Come..."

"Come!"

"*Come!*"

"I said shut up!" Lev roared, halting his forward motion and snapping himself back to his senses.

The whispering stopped.

"Finally. Guess that explains where most of the others went."

Gherm resurfaced. *Most?*

We've worked with Hemgall and... cooperated with Vyrga enough to know those two wouldn't fall for this trick, Lev explained. *You should know neither of them are simple-minded fools. Fools rarely get to lead others and make something of themselves. And I'm sure some of the other captives should be able to handle a situation like this.*

So where did... they go? Why... leave us?

Lev shrugged and looked to his right. *Don't know about Vyrga or Hemgall, but I bet the other captives have gone in the other direction to get as far away from that thing as possible. Though it is likely that there would be other dangers over there. We need to get down from here to investigate first.*

And... Rapha?

Yeah, I'm bringing her along, Lev replied. He hoisted her up and draped her over his shoulder. "Let's go, shall we?" he said to both the unconscious girl and his spiritual companion before slowly and carefully climbing down the giant insect's carcass.

Using the light from the crystal, he searched around the hiveling's corpse for any abandoned equipment and any sign of his missing companions.

He kept searching around till he stumbled on some footprints and a broken bottle of pitch. Lev examined the label—it was one of his.

Thieves... Gherm whispered.

Really? Who would've guessed? Lev replied. He returned his attention to the footprints. *Don't take it so seriously. Thieves peeve me and I've been having trouble controlling my emotions in this body.*

It's... my body...

You mean our *body. At least 'til I find a better alternative.*

Thief...

Lev chuckled. *I am, aren't I? Though I didn't want to live once again as a member of a marginalized class, now, did I? How ironic... I tried my best to free myself and those I care about from oppression only to fall right back to the bottom.* He remembered that Gherm was listening to him think. *Don't worry, though. You should be able to guess that I don't plan on staying like this.*

Becoming a leader... isn't enough? Gherm's voice resonated with a rawness Lev had not foreseen from his disembodied host. *You're now... a greyborn! How high... do you want to fly... before you... fall!*

Don't be a coward, Gherm. I'm planning something big and you should know it.

Ghorza will be hurt! Gherm yelled.

No, she won't. I'll make sure she stays out of this. That part you should already know.

Why take... things slow... then? Why be... friendly to Rak?

It takes time to train men and gather resources and it takes alliances to fight society.

But—

I don't plan to take over the world. I only plan to free it.

Why him?

Look, I know you're angry that you can't control this body, but couldn't you at least pay attention for once? Rak's more trustworthy than others, his men are reliable, and as long as I don't break the contract and try to usurp him, I can be sure he'll follow your people's code and not stab me in the back, Lev ranted. *You know, for thugs, you greyborns are quite honorable. An act for an act, and loyalty for loyalty... Though I guess greyborns wouldn't want to kill each other too often. Class solidarity is a wonderful thing.*

Fine...

Let's try finding a way out for now. We should at least find some food, water, and a place to rest before she wakes up, yeah?

Gherm paused for a moment before Lev felt him calm down. *Let's...*

Good. Posture relaxed, Lev proceeded to search for a path out of the abyss.

CHAPTER 21
EDGE OF TOMORROW

A few hours had passed since Lev had regained consciousness. He could only find one path out of the room, at least within the boundaries of the area he allowed himself to explore. Only in case he found no other solution would he have explored where the whispers tried to guide him.

Despite his weariness, he kept his eyes focused on any nasty surprises which might have occured while he marched forward, Rapha draped over his left shoulder. The only times he stopped were when he needed to take a momentary break to replenish his strength and rest his aching feet.

Finally, something to drink! he silently rejoiced as he came upon the underground lake before his eyes. He gently placed Rapha and the haze crystal on the ground before he removed his helmet and dipped it in the water to use as a bucket.

He shone the light of the crystal into the water to check for any anomalies before he raised the helmet to his face and sniffed for any odours. *Hmm, smells like sweat. Does that mean the water's safe? There could be some harmful minerals...*

He stared into the water, resisting the urge to lick his cracked lips. *There aren't any corpses nearby or any signs of struggles from suffocation or paralysis. But my allies have my waterskins, so they could have drunk from those instead...*

As Lev contemplated whether he should risk drinking from the lake, he heard a weary cracked voice from behind.

"W-what happened? Where... am I?" Rapha asked. She tried to move her splinted arms to get up, but winced in pain.

"My arms... I can't move them! What happened to my—" She erupted into a fit of dry coughs.

Lev dropped the helmet on the ground and rushed to her side. "Easy! Calm down!"

"How do you expect me to calm down! My arms were shattered by a bloody insect! And why can I barely feel them!"

"I've applied some medicine to save the nerves. We'll get you healed up when we reconvene with the others."

Rapha chuckled ruefully. "Please, Lev. You know they won't heal me. Even if I do survive, I'll be nothing but a liability. I'll either end up a sex slave or be tossed aside to die like the expendable I am." She chuckled ever more, and before long, her chuckles turned to cries. "I'm doomed. Damned and doomed! It would be better for me to drown myself now..."

"Yeah, no. I don't think so."

"Why, though? I'm useless. There's no way we could convince Bulgu's healers to fix my arms."

"Who said anything about needing help from that bastard and his pawns?"

"Is there anyone else who would heal me?"

Lev lay down on his back next to her and let his own arms flop at his sides, knees pointed at the ceiling. "I have contacts. It will probably take a lot longer, but I assure you, I'll get you fixed up."

"What makes you so sure?"

Lev turned his head to face Rapha. "I'm sure because I know myself and I know my capabilities. Healers in bogey-kind aren't rare—they just don't usually choose to treat greyborns like me. But like I said, I have contacts."

Rapha sat silently for a while, gazing down at Lev. Without warning, she abruptly looked away, but not before Lev glimpsed a sparkle return to her eyes. "If you manage to do that, I'd do anything. Heck, I'd even marry you."

Lev grimaced. "I wouldn't offer that last thing so lightly if I were you."

"A life for a life. You'd be saving me from a dog's death, you know."

"So you did mean it. It's true that you'll owe me your life, but that doesn't have to mean marriage or slavery."

"How so?"

"I just find it distasteful."

A moment passed between the two. "Then what do you want instead?"

"Loyalty, without chains, and knowledge would suffice. Once we're out, teach me all you know about the outside world and help me take down those who stand in my way. I want you to be a companion who'd question my actions and guide me when I'm wrong, not a trained war hound who'd commit any atrocities I'd tell them to."

"So you want me to be a part of your council? Your war-maiden?" Rapha asked excitedly.

"That's one way to put it. If I heal you, would you agree to that?"

"Definitely!" she yelled giddily enough to nearly forget the pain in her arms—that is, before she overestimated her ability to stand up by herself and underestimated how parched her throat was.

"Here, let me help," Lev told the girl while helping her stand.

"Thank you," the goblin girl said with a blush.

"No problem."

"By the way, do you have any water? My supplies were with the carriers..." She watched the corners of Lev's mouth drop.

Lev stood quiet for a while. "Sadly, no. We've been robbed."

"You're kidding me."

"I wish I was. Thankfully they left my equipment alone. Specifically my helmet."

She looked towards the headgear lying on the ground with water trickling out of the ear holes. "You used it as a bucket, right? Though looking at you, it doesn't look like you've drunk from it."

"I'm not sure if the water's safe to drink yet."

"Lev, if we don't risk it and drink, we might not find another water source. Where are we by the way? This doesn't look like the 7th floor."

Lev hesitated. "We're in uncharted territory."

"What? Did I hear that right?" Rapha asked, flabbergasted.

"You did."

"Great. Just great. Then what do we do now? How do we get back up with no supplies, no weapons, half our party unable to fight, and giant bugs waiting to kill us?"

"By being careful and paying attention to our surroundings. So far we haven't encountered any hivelings." He paused as he gathered information from Gherm's memories. "And we have an escape route. On every floor, there are certain shrines that can teleport you to other shrines on the floors above."

"There are? Then why aren't they being used?"

"For two reasons. The first is that the shrines can only teleport small groups, no more than ten at a time. The second is that the shrines above the third floor were destroyed a long time ago. When the Jiira first started exploring the cavern, they foolishly destroyed the portals, thinking they were icons of false gods. The only reason the other portals were safe is that a scouting group once went ahead of the expeditionary force and accidentally activated shrine teleportation while trying to run away with treasure."

"The Jiira must be the foulest, most undisciplined, and most sacrilegious fools I've ever met," Rapha growled.

"Descendants of the Enlightened One or not, it's a wonder they became strong enough to rule others in the first place."

"True. By the way, can you please help me drink? I'm dying of thirst, so just let me test it for the both of us."

"Are you sure?"

"Yes, I'm sure, and even if I wasn't, this isn't the time to be paranoid."

Lev took off his helmet and scooped out a helmet-full of water, then took off his robe.

"What in the world are you doing!"

He bent down near the lake and washed his robe "Cleaning my clothes. The water seems to have been formed from water dripping off of speleothems, so it should be safe for washing and drinking. I'd prefer to boil the water, but beggars can't be choosers."

As he washed his clothes, he pointed at his helmet, which he'd placed on the ground. "There. Let's see if it's drinkable, shall we?" he asked the flustered Rapha.

"Y-Yeah."

After wringing out his shirt, Lev helped Rapha raise his helmet to her lips, and she drank.

Lev stared at her in silence, trying to observe any change in her behavior. Rapha stared back, shoulders tensed and lips pursed, trying not to fixate on his toned chest.

"Looks like it's safe to drink. Hopefully."

"Hopefully?"

"Never mind." He sipped from the helmet and refilled it again.

"*Hopefully*, we'll find something to eat," retorted Rapha.

"We may. So let's continue looking for our thieves, shall we?"

"We're also looking for thieves?"

"Are you proposing that we just give them our equipment? Depending on the reason, a few extra hands might be welcome. And that's a big 'might'—I'm more in the mood to dish out some punishment—but we do need numbers to survive."

"Then let's go already."

Lev nodded. "Let's go."

* * *

What felt like a few hours had passed since they had resumed walking. The path was now lit with numerous large, bright haze crystals, revealing pockets of other magical stones and various signs of life.

As they approached a corner, Lev suddenly stopped to inspect the wall.

"What is it?" asked Rapha.

"Nothing. Just thinking we should prepare ourselves beforehand. Who knows what could be hiding on the other side?" Lev took out his knife.

Rapha shined her haze crystal on the ground and spotted an unusually dark spot further ahead near the left wall of the path, devoid of crystal growth and seemingly absorbing light. She pointed it out to Lev. "What's that?"

"Stay here. It's probably a trap." Lev drew his blade.

"Most likely, but I don't think staying here would be to my advantage. If there's something out there, it would most likely want to separate us."

Lev stuck his left arm out to block Rapha's advance. "Or it could want to kill us both at the same time."

"I still think it's better for me to come with you," Rapha insisted. "I could at least save myself the trouble of being a hostage."

"I might use you as a shield if you come."

"Doesn't matter. If you're killed, I'm next."

Lev lowered his arm. "Suit yourself." Gripping his knife tightly in his right hand, legs tensed to jump backwards in case of any sudden movement, he advanced towards the object while repeatedly scanning his surroundings.

"Seems we've found our first victim," he said.

He crouched next to the freshly-mangled corpse of a young-looking, yellow bogey. Judging by the way he had held his now-haze-coated focus amulet, Lev concluded that the bogey must have been a shaman in the life that this unknown assailant had stolen from him. Judging by the wear on his clothes, he must have hailed from the areas bordering the slums.

His body lay between two stalagmites. His right arm was ripped from the shoulder blade, his freshly concave skull was missing its lower jaw, his tongue lolled out, and his kneecaps were shattered. His abdominal cavity was split open, but his entrails were missing.

"W-What could've done this?" whimpered Rapha.

"We'll know soon enough."

"Wha—"

"On my mark, jump to the side."

Rapha could only come to one conclusion. "It's above us, isn't it?"

"Now!"

They both immediately leapt away from the corpse before it was smashed by an abominable figure.

Rapha quickly identified the figure: it was Drogg. Yet it was not exactly Drogg—his formerly red skin was now purplish grey with cysts sprouting all over. His form was three times larger. A gigantic plant-like bulb on his back spouted noxious gas. The bulb had dug roots into his body, poking out of all his orifices, starting with a beard of tentacles and ending with a tail of vines.

"I told you to come... I would have made you perfect... But it seems you have chosen death," spoke the abomination in multiple dissonant voices.

"It seems we did," said Lev, stance steady, head tilted, and attention on a particularly enthralling stalactite.

"Good. Let's end this quickly," replied Drogg.

Suddenly a horrible screech filled the area. Drogg's back had been set ablaze.

Lev side-eyed Drogg without moving his head. "I never said this would be *our* end."

A clay bottle sailed through the air and shattered against the creature's bulb. Drogg screeched louder.

Hemgall, Shahn, another deka, and two greyborns emerged from the darkness and charged at the monster. Hemgall and the deka dodged a swing of its arm and chopped down at it. The other greyborns repeatedly stabbed at the burning bulb with spears, setting the pitch-covered heads alight and burning the insides of the bulb.

From deeper in the darkness, another pitch bottle and a fireball collided with the beast concurrently. The beast wailed, trying to retaliate with its roots and tendrils, which burned to ash upon emerging from its body.

As the flames spread into the creature's torso, the beast fell to the ground, moaning and writhing, vines charring and skin singing.

"That ends that," said Lev, hardly batting an eyelid.

Rapha choked out a few words. "How did— Where did—"

Lev chuckled. "Hemgall carved my group's sign for ambush on the wall."

"And good thing I *did*. We managed to take care of the last of these things!"

Her eyes widened. "You've fought them before?"

"We have. Fortunately, it was easy to take them down once we discovered their weakness to fire. If only the torches hadn't scared them so easily, they could've been a challenge," Vyrga replied with a smirk once he emerged from the darkness along with a green bogey.

"The unfortunate part is that *that* bastard had to survive," said Hemgall.

Vyrga turned to face the large greyborn. "Not as unfortunate as your sense of humour. Considering your... intelligence, I expected you to join them instead of following me ahead."

"I followed you because I knew you were up to no good."

"Hah, no. I'm no fool. Infighting would currently be the death of us all. Fools would be the ones who choose to follow you."

"Really? I thought fools were like that shaman you coerced. And he paid for it with his life, didn't he?"

"We needed bait."

"We did not! You just wasted what could have been a valuable asset in combat."

"Better safe than sorry. We both know he just wanted to make off with our supplies."

Hemgall laughed. "That's funny, you talking about trust. He might've been a thief, but you stole some of Lev's stuff, too. Oh, and here you go by the way," said Hemgall, walking over to Lev and pulling out Lev's marching pack. "I managed to convince the others to leave the rest of your stuff alone."

"Thanks." Lev inspected his belongings. His shield and spear were both operational, but his pack seemed to be missing some items.

Lev turned to Vyrga. "Now would you kindly return the rest? I seem to be missing a few bottles of pitch and medications."

Vyrga sneered. "Sadly, I can't. As you've just seen, we needed them to deal with these aberrations. I assure you, I'll repay you once we return to safe grounds."

"And you expect me to trust you?"

"I expect you to be logical and refrain from doing anything that might compromise our odds of escape."

Lev and Vyrga stared each other in the eyes, but neither backed down. They stayed like that till Rapha coughed, grabbing their attention.

"So what's happening right now?" Rapha asked while looking at the now shimmering corpse.

Lev spoke without looking away from Vyrga. "The remains will disappear soon—don't ask me how. They just turn into balls of light and vanish into the walls. Even our shaman friend—"

"How many times should I tell you the name's Orva?" the shaman cut in.

"As many times I need to tell others not to interrupt me when I'm talking, girl," Vyrga replied.

Orva threw her arms up. "Do it right the first time and I won't interrupt you."

Vyrga continued. "Even our friend Orva here doesn't know how that happens. Don't think about it too much. It's just another mystery of this place."

"I see. So are we staying here or are we going to eat something and continue ahead?" she asked.

Everyone turned silent.

Hemgall sighed. "Well, you see... we found a giant gate with a golden door, but we can't seem to open it no matter what we do."

"A gate?" replied Rapha.

"It's not far from here. It'd be better if you two saw it. It's also better to eat there since there's also light, edible plants, and water," Shahn interjected.

"There is, huh... Could it be a trap?"

"It's not. We made sure of that. We also checked everywhere else. There's no other path but that one."

"In that case, we'd better go there now. Maybe we can find a way to open it, and even if we don't, we still need a proper place to rest."

Everyone nodded and proceeded towards the door.

As Shahn had said, it didn't take long for them to reach the gate. Both Lev and Rapha felt their jaws drop.

"Magnificent, isn't it?" Hemgall said as he gazed at the glorious marble figure.

The figure was eight killigs tall. Along the gate were engraved, unknown sagas describing forgotten gods and tales detailing what Lev assumed was the creation of the world, its evolution, and a great cataclysmic war that would've torn the world apart. There were detailed portraits of all kinds of creatures, both magic and mundane. There were even depictions of goblins, bogeys, and hivelings preparing to face off in battle.

"What... is this?" Rapha muttered. "Is everything predicted here?"

The shaman scoffed. "I believe it's nonsense. It looks like bogeys and hivelings are fighting together against your goblin kin. Utterly ridiculous."

"It could also just be the Jiira," she countered.

"Could be," replied Hemgall in the shaman's place. "But I can't fathom us fighting alongside those bugs."

Lev cut in. "More importantly, let's see if we can open it." He approached the golden door. Though it was not as magnificent as the gate, it was stunning in its own right, engraved with symbols in an unknown language and adorned with depictions of nine masks, each with a different color of gems for eyes—red, orange, yellow, green, blue, indigo, violet, black, and white. All of the masks were small except the white-eyed one positioned in the centre of the gate.

Everyone closed in on Lev to see what he would do.

There doesn't seem to be a lock, he noted. *Let's see if there's some sort of mechanism hidden behind one of these decorations.*

He touched the gate. Blindingly white light burst forth from the central mask and engulfed his surroundings. Lev covered his eyes and screamed in pain.

"I thought you said there were no traps!"

Lev heard no response. He uncovered his eyes and looked back—not only was nobody there, but also the scenery had changed. There was nothing but the void. Even the gate was gone. In its place was a giant figure covered with an intricate white robe, glowing white eyes piercing through a white mask.

Leonard Erand Vandersteen, I've been waiting for you, said a voice echoing inside his head.

What— Gherm? No—who are *you?* he cried.

An ancient holy man once sent out a letter to all that could read: the oppressed, the noble, and the ones fighting for the glory of their nation. This letter, blessed by that man, was sent out to all the nations that believed in him. It asked for change, a new beginning, and a better tomorrow. A true global revolution...

"What are you reading, Leonard?" asked Eric, peeking at the ancient bundle of documents hastily bound together.

"Nothing, Eric," Leo replied. Eric did not need to know about things that did not concern him.

Eric pointed at a photo sticking out from the bundled stack of documents. "Who's that?"

"She's... an old friend of mine, back when I was in Neue Berlin as a kid." She had fled Eurasia at the age of eighteen. The only thing Lev knew about her now was that she had become one of the Emperor's hands, the select few who assisted the Emperor himself in ruling his vast empire in the West. "I'll see her again... soon."

"Soon? What do you mean, Leo?"

"It's nothing, Eric. Just drop it. We still have to report our losses from the previous battles... We can't let General von Loden wait— we've lost way too many men to slack on this report."

Despite his insistence that they return to work, the photo distracted him. *Know that we will meet again soon, Maria,* he whispered under his breath. *We can free this world again. Let's write our world's history— ourselves.*

Just like Eric said, I'll become a lord by my own hands.

AFTERWORD

Hey everyone,

This first installment took us longer than expected to finish so we want to thank all of you as well as our readers at RoyalRoad, ScribbleHub, and Webnovel for their patience!

However, we want you to know this story is far from over.

That's why, we hope you'll continue to support us throughout our journey as we work on future releases of the series as well.

We want to give our special thanks to Miko, Lan, and their team for the amazing artwork. Without you, it would've been impossible to bring the world within our novel to life!

And finally, we'd also like to give a big *hooray* to MoonQuill and their publishing team, with a special, well-deserved thanks to Nadine for her amazing editing skills and feedback. We're grateful to all of you for the services you have provided us with from start to finish.

Thanks, everyone, for being part of this project.

We hope you enjoyed reading *Lord of Goblins*!

Michiel & Hadi

ABOUT US

Michiel Werbrouck

Michiel Werbrouck started out writing short, science-fiction, horror stories on various online platforms until he found the courage to write and submit one of his first one-shot web novels online.

He started writing Lord of Goblins together with Hadi in late 2019 and has since been expanding the series together with Hadi. Influences from his and Hadi's previous works can still be found in this new, co-authored series.

In his free time you can find him playing various grand strategy games, reading novels, and programming games/applications.

Hadi Y. Bendakji

Hadi Y. Bendakji found joy in reading and writing from an early age. Taking part in literary art allowed him to express himself and he soon started writing on Quizilla, but it was short-lived due to an increase in school activities.

In more recent years, Hadi found further encouragement from countless novels and he decided to try his hand at a new project—a world creation novel. In 2019, he met Michiel and the two decided to write *Lord of Goblins*, and they've vowed to keep working on the series until it reaches the ending it deserves, which won't be any time soon.

Hadi studied software development and his hobbies include reading, writing, programming, and listening to metal, especially songs by DA Games.

Vu Dinh Lan

Vu Dinh Lan is the lead artist at Darkness Comics. He created the smash-hit, crowdfunded, Vietnamese manga series *Project ICON*, and has won a Silent Manga Audition award for best silent manga in 2015.

Lan likes to collect his ideas during short breaks at coffee shops or at his old school as it helps him focus on drawing. You can usually find him listening to Script, 911, Backstreet Boys, and My Chemical Romance whilst drawing.

Darkness Comics

Darkness Comics started out as a comic club in 2012 and has recently turned into an indie manga and webtoon studio based in Vietnam. They have been providing their services to countless clients worldwide since 2019.

All illustrations in this volume were done by Vu Dinh Lan and his assistants at Darkness Comics.

MoonQuill

MoonQuill is an original story hosting platform and indie publisher created by writers. This up-and-coming community strives to shorten the serialization and monetization process for authors while providing readers with a world of original content for their continued enjoyment.

Printed in Great Britain
by Amazon